"Ou... ...o Me...

To us. Th... ...ly for us to share."

Cara's eyes slid closed. Alex was saying all the right things. "Oh, Alex."

"I mean it, Cara."

Cara didn't know what to say to that. She berated herself for believing him. For thinking that possibly, he was telling the truth this time. The problem was, she didn't know where take Alex ended and the real Alex began.

Her silence brought forth his deep sigh. "I can't change what happened between us, Cara. If I could, I would. But I hope your heart tells you to give us another chance."

Cara nibbled on her lower lip. "This is very hard for me, Alex."

Queasiness rocked her belly, but she didn't think it was Baby del Toro causing the turmoil this time—it was the little one's father.

The Texas Renegade Returns
is a *Texas Cattleman's Club: The Missing Mogul*
novel. Love and scandal meet in Royal, Texas!

* * *

If you're on Twitter,
tell us what you think of Harlequin Desire!
#harlequindesire

Dear Reader,

I hope you are enjoying the Texas Cattleman's Club: The Missing Mogul series! In this book, the ninth and final story in this wonderful continuity, you'll see Alejandro aka Alex del Toro as he was meant to be— the main character and true hero of the story.

The Texas Renegade has returned!

With his memory back, Alex is a driven man and has plans to get Cara Windsor, his one and only love, to forgive his deception and fall back into his arms. He also hopes to make amends with the friends he's betrayed at the Cattleman's Club. Then there's the issue of Alex finding the culprit who had him kidnapped and shanghaied over the Mexican border.

Cara Windsor is no pushover; she has a secret of her own and is now wiser in the precariousness of love. Alex's betrayal weighs heavily on her and she has a difficult time believing in the man she'd once adored. But oh, how she wishes things were different between them. Alex's deep dark eyes and beautiful smile still make her heart strum.

I instantly fell in love with Alex del Toro (and hope you do, too) as I discovered his patience and commitment in trying to win Cara back. He's a man who's not perfect, a man who's made a mistake, but he's also a man who knows exactly what he wants. I hope you enjoy reading how the sexy renegade persuades a cautious Cara to give him a second chance.

The one thing I do guarantee you: a happily ever after—Texas Cattleman's Club style!

Happy Reading!

Charlene Sands

THE
TEXAS RENEGADE
RETURNS

—

CHARLENE SANDS

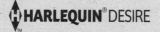

HARLEQUIN® DESIRE

Special thanks and acknowledgment to Charlene Sands
for her contribution to the
Texas Cattleman's Club: The Missing Mogul miniseries.

Recycling programs
for this product may
not exist in your area.

ISBN-13: 978-0-373-73301-9

THE TEXAS RENEGADE RETURNS

H HARLEQUIN®
TM www.Harlequin.com

Printed in U.S.A.

Books by Charlene Sands

Harlequin Desire

Silhouette Desire

Harlequin Historical

Other titles by this author
available in ebook format.

CHARLENE SANDS

is a *USA TODAY* bestselling author of thirty-five romance novels, writing sensual contemporary romances and stories of the Old West. Her books have been honored with a National Readers' Choice Award, a Cataromance Reviewers' Choice Award, and she's a double recipient of the Booksellers' Best Award. She belongs to the Orange County chapter and the Los Angeles chapter of RWA.

Charlene writes "hunky heroes with heart." She knows a little something about true romance—she married her high school sweetheart! When not writing, Charlene enjoys sunny Pacific beaches, great coffee, reading books from her favorite authors and spending time with her family. You can find her on Facebook and Twitter. Charlene loves to hear from her readers! You can write her at P.O. Box 4883, West Hills, CA 91308 or sign up for her newsletter for fun blogs and ongoing contests at www.charlenesands.com.

To my sister Carol...my best friend.

One

"I'm terribly sorry Mr. del Toro, but Miss Windsor is very busy right now. She can't see you today."

Alex stared at Cara's assistant who didn't sound sorry at all. She sat stiff-shouldered behind her Plexiglas desk in the austere offices of Windsor Energy like a mama bear protecting her cub. She was doing her job, so he couldn't blame her for that, but that Wicked Witch of the West glare she was giving him had to go.

Now that the truth about his real identity was out, friendly faces in Royal, Texas, were a rare commodity. You'd think he'd sprouted gills and swam with piranha. Old man Windsor had probably alerted his security staff to usher him out of the building on sight. He'd deal with Paul Windsor another time. Today, he'd come for Cara and he wasn't leaving Windsor Energy without her.

He darted his gaze at Cara's office door. *Dios,* he was dying to see her. He had things to tell her that could not wait.

He aimed his best smile straight at the middle-aged assistant. As a boy in Mexico, his natural charm had served him well and he'd learned how to get around his schoolteachers and later, as a young man, he'd perfected the art of persuasion with the opposite sex. Now, the only woman he cared about persuading was Cara Windsor.

"Miss," he said, verifying the woman's name by her nameplate, "Miss Potter, you look like a reasonable woman and I would never want you to risk your job, so perhaps you can simply let Miss Windsor know I'm here. Or, I can take it upon myself to open her door unannounced. I don't think Miss Windsor would appreciate the intrusion and I really don't want to barge in, but one way or another," he said, gesturing toward Cara's door, "I will be seeing her today." He kept his smile from wavering.

Miss Potter's shoulders gave an inch. Her eyes begged for understanding. "I'm supposed to call Security if you should ever show up here."

"You don't want to do that, do you?"

"No, but Mr. Windsor issued the order. And everyone knows…"

"What do they know?"

Her gaze dipped to the desktop. "That you broke Cara's heart."

Ouch! Miss Potter didn't mince words. This was just a taste of what he was up against.

"I can assure you, I am not going to hurt Cara, so rather than get you in trouble for not doing your job, let us just pretend I didn't stop by your desk. I will just let myself into her—"

"Gayle? What's going on here?"

Cara's lilting voice drifted from the doorway. It smoothed all of his rough edges and calmed him down inside. He pivoted on his heels and turned around.

Seeing Cara's beautiful face tore him up inside. She had one slender hand on the edge of the door, her body half in, half out of the doorway. The fluorescents shimmered over her straight blond hair and cascaded over her shoulders as smooth as golden honey. Memories came to mind of those soft silky locks teasing over his face as she made love to him right after he'd been released from the hospital.

Today, she wore a business suit of slate-gray, nothing special, nothing noteworthy, but on her, it looked like a *Vogue* fashion cover. His gaze drifted to her white blouse underneath, clinging to her skin and dipping into the valley between her breasts.

How he missed her.

Her eyes rounded on him and the sparkle in those blue gems faded. Breath rushed out of her like a hiss. "Alex, what are you doing here?" So much for *smooth* and *lilting*.

"I came for you."

She began shaking her head and set her chin firmly. "You can't be here."

Gayle Potter rose from her seat. "I'm sorry, Miss Windsor. I tried to stop him."

"She did. She tried to stop me. But as you know—"

"You're not stoppable, when you want something." Her mouth pulled down, sweeping away any welcome on her face.

He had a lot of making up to do.

"It's okay, Gayle," she said. "I understand."

"Should I call S-Security?"

Cara's chest rose and fell and she sighed. "No, I'll handle this. If you could excuse us a moment and take your break, I'll walk Mr. *del Toro* out."

He cringed at the bitterness spewing from her lips. He was here to rectify his mistakes, not hurt her anymore.

Gayle darted a worried glance at both of them as she grabbed her bag and scooted out of the office. "Certainly, I'll be in the lounge if you need me."

"You shouldn't even be in this building," Cara was saying.

"Huh? Oh, what?" He found himself staring and following her every movement. His memories of her didn't do her justice. He hadn't seen her for weeks and he'd almost forgotten the blue sparkle in her pretty eyes, like the ocean when first touched by morning sun. He'd almost forgotten the round full shape of her breasts. And legs that made him want to weep when they wrapped around him.

She'd made him laugh, too. They'd do the silliest things together and act like kids without a care in the world. No wonder he'd fallen so hard and fast for her.

"I said...you need to leave."

"I'll leave as soon as you agree to come with me. We need to talk."

Her expression hardened, and she gazed at him as if he were nothing more than a stranger. But he wasn't a stranger. He was still the same man. If he could only convince her of that. He couldn't accept that it was over between them. He'd explain and apologize, but first, he had one other thing to do.

"I don't know you, Alex del Toro," she said. "I thought I knew you, back when I was foolish and so naive. The Alex Santiago I fell in love with and planned to marry was sweet and caring. He and I clicked. But that's not who you are, is it? You're not Alex Santiago. It was all a lie. Everything about you is a lie. You used me and, what's saddest of all, you don't remember any of it. If you did, you wouldn't be standing here today asking to see me. You'd know it's pointless, amnesia or not."

"Cara," he said. "It's not pointless. Come with me. I promise it won't take long." He'd blown it with her big-time, but it wasn't going to end this way. He glanced at her left hand. She wasn't wearing his engagement ring. His stomach nose-dived with dread. She hated him.

With wary eyes, she glanced down the hallway that led to the main entry. "My father's due back in the office in ten minutes. If he sees you here, he'll have you dragged out of the building."

Alex took his best shot. He had nothing else to lose. More than restoring his good name to his friends and col-leagues in the county, he needed Cara to hear him out. To believe in him again. "Then why create a scene here where you work? I'm only asking for an hour of your time. I promise to deposit you right back here when we're through." Or not. If things went as planned, Alex would be taking her to his home in Pine Valley.

An exasperated sigh fell from her lips. She glanced at her watch, then at the front doorway again. He didn't know it, but Paul Windsor was helping Alex win back Cara. "Okay," she said softly. "I'll go with you, but only because my father's blood pressure will explode if he sees you."

Dios, that took some doing.

As for Paul Windsor, if Alex's suspicions were correct, the man with four ex-wives wouldn't be available to marry a fifth wife. He'd be in prison.

On kidnapping and attempted-murder charges.

"Give me a minute, Alex. I'll meet you outside. Where are you parked?"

"First red Ferrari you see in the parking lot." He smiled. She'd helped him pick out the car. Red was her favorite color. He remembered that about her, too.

He remembered almost everything now.

* * *

Cara leaned over her desk and scribbled a quick note to Gayle, telling her not to say a word to anyone about Alex. She also told her loyal assistant not to worry.

If only she wasn't worried. She had her doubts about going with Alex. Months ago, he'd disappeared right after their engagement. There had been no sign of him anywhere and at first she'd pretty much panicked. Alex wouldn't have left without saying something to her. He wouldn't have given her an engagement ring, pledged undying love and then walked away. She'd held on to the hope that he'd forgotten to tell her he was going on a business trip where he couldn't be reached. But she'd never heard back from him. Days had turned into weeks. No one had heard from him. As soon as he'd proposed to her, Alex had disappeared. Many people had speculated that his disappearance was suspicious and there was some sort of foul play involved. Some had been sure he was the victim of a crime. Initially, Cara had believed the same.

But as time wore on, she'd secretly feared Alex had run out on her because he didn't love her enough. Crazy thoughts and doubts entered her head. She'd lived under a constant sense of self-torture. Alex regretted his decision to marry her. Alex had gone back to an ex-lover. She wasn't the woman for him and he didn't have the courage to tell her.

Cara sighed as she glanced at the tall, dark and dangerously handsome man staring at her with eyes gleaming. She, along with the rest of the world, now knew the truth.

Alex had been discovered among a group of immigrants sneaking into the United States after their truck collided with another car. It was all one big mystery and Alex claimed amnesia. He didn't remember much of his disappearance. But he'd had serious injuries, including a concussion and broken wrist from the collision. Cara had thought the worst about him and lived with guilt for weeks, scolding herself for thinking he'd run out on her. Fool that she was, she'd tried everything she could think of to bring back his memory while he was in the hospital. Nothing had worked.

Cara walked out of her office, her heels furiously clicking against sleek gray-slate floors. She had no time to spare. Her father was due back any minute and those were fireworks she never wanted to see.

Stepping outside, Texas sunlight poured over her. She slipped on her sunglasses and scoured around. Alex was hard to miss. She found him leaning against his slick red sports car, his arms crossed and his black hair catching light rays. He was wearing black trousers, a soft white shirt and a devastating smile. Cara's breath caught again. It happened every time she laid eyes on him.

Fraud, she kept shouting in her head.

Yet, her heart pinged at the sight of him.

Alex Santiago had never really existed and the truth had broken her heart. He was Alejandro del Toro, only son and heir to Del Toro Oil, who'd come from Mexico to spy on their biggest rivals, Windsor Energy. Alex had created a false identity, lived for over a year in Maverick County posing as Alex Santiago and had used her as a pawn to extract information about her father's successful oil business. The truth came to light after Alex was discovered alive and brought back to town. Concerned about his son's health and hoping to help him recover from amnesia, Rodrigo del Toro revealed to the world Alex's true identity and the real reason he'd come to Texas in the first place—to spy on Windsor Oil.

The burn of that betrayal still seared her with pain.

It didn't matter that Alex couldn't remember any of it.

His amnesia didn't make him any less guilty. Her father had never liked her choice of fiancé and he'd been right all along about Alex. That was the biggest crime. Her father, who'd been married and divorced four times, had better insight about Alex than she did.

What a fool she'd been.

She left three feet of pavement between them. "I really don't want to do this."

"I know. I appreciate your time."

He came forward to wind his hand around hers and lead her to the passenger-side door. Her palms grew damp from his touch. His strength and power was always a big turn-on. How she'd loved him once.

A part of her was glad he had amnesia. A part of her wished she had it, too.

She stood by the open door. "Where are we going?"

His eyes were nearly black. When they made love, she would slowly sink into them. "You'll see. I won't harm you, Cara. I'm still the same Alex you knew."

Not true. She didn't argue with him though. She slipped into the leather seat and fastened her seat belt. Alex got behind the wheel and pulled out of the parking lot.

He was quiet on the drive. It was fine with her. She relaxed back against the seat and stared out the front window. For about three minutes. Then her gaze slid from the highway to his handsome face. His profile alone could sell magazines to millions of women. She forced her eyes back to the road.

Don't remember his hands caressing your body. Don't remember his mouth pressing yours. Don't remember the scent of his hot skin when he was aroused and ready to make love to you.

Beautiful memories clicked away in her mind. Her head ached with them. She didn't want to believe him a liar, user, fraud and spy. But he was all those things. And here she was, sitting beside him, giving him her time and using her father as the excuse to steal away with him.

Cara, you dumbass.

Alex made a right turn off the highway that led away from town. Storefronts and residential streets gave way to the open road. Tight muscles in her neck began to relax. Rolling her shoulders, her stiffness dropped away there, too. She came alive in the country. Across the flatlands, ranches came into view. Roadside wildflowers bursting with color sprouted up along the miles and miles of fences.

Alex hit the controls and the windows rolled all the way down. Gentle springtime breezes replaced the air-conditioning. Her hair blew into her eyes. She didn't bother trying to fix the mass of blond whipping at her cheeks.

"Now, please close your eyes."

"Why?"

A few strands of his black hair danced across his forehead as he smiled—a dashing-marauder kind of smile. "Because I asked you nicely."

She didn't want to do him any favors, but she'd agreed to this. One hour was all the time she would give him, and twenty of those minutes were already up. She closed her eyes.

"Thank you," he said.

Those two softly spoken words squeezed tight inside her heart.

Not long after, he parked the car. "Keep them closed," he said.

The swooshing of quiet waters drifted into her ears. Distant music played and her nostrils were hit with crisp fresh air. "For how long?"

"Until I tell you to open them."

The driver's-side door clicked closed and his footfalls

grew louder as he approached her side. The door opened and his scent of woods and musk invaded her senses. His subtle cologne meant only for her, he would say, stirred her into restlessness. He brushed her body to help with the seat belt and snap, her heart, as well as her seat belt, were undone. She shifted in her seat.

"Won't be long now," he assured her, his melodic voice reaching her ears. It was the same tone he'd used when he told her he loved her. He was so near. So close. Her breath hitched in her throat and she swallowed.

He reached for her hand and helped her out of the car. "Careful, Cara."

Darn it, she was trying to be. With him.

Under her heels, small stones and uneven ground kept her unsteady, but Alex's firm grip wouldn't allow her to fall. "I'd carry you if you'd let me."

"Not even in your dreams. How much farther?"

"Almost there."

A sinking ache in the pit of her stomach warned her that this wasn't a good idea. The road they'd traveled, the scent in the air, the quietly rushing waters, gave credence to her rising suspicions.

The ground under her feet was softer now, her ankles tickled by fragrant wisps of flowers.

Alex stopped and announced, "You can open your eyes now."

Her eyelids lifted. A beam of sunlight caressed a quiet river. She stood in a field of bluebonnets, the cushion under her feet. Alex took her shoulders and turned her around. She blinked and gazed out. Wooden stakes outlined the skeletal beginnings of a country house Alex had promised to build for her. Inside the house, in what was to be a dining room facing the river, a table was set for two with a floral centerpiece of ivy and gardenias. A quartet of musicians stood off to the side, playing Alex and Cara's favorite songs.

She didn't get it. Why had he brought her here? This was where Alex had proposed to her. From childhood, she'd loved this little patch of land where bluebonnets carpeted the banks of the river and mesquite trees grew tall and shady.

When Alex had been in the hospital recovering from his injuries, Cara spent time with him, trying to get him to remember her. Trying to revive his memory about the special love they'd shared. She'd told him of his beautiful marriage proposal and how it had filled her heart with joy. The way he'd proposed had shown her that he'd paid attention. He'd known what she loved. He'd known what little things made her happy.

She'd been desperate to rekindle his memory. She'd been desperate for him to remember their love. But that was back when Cara believed he was Alex Santiago and not a spy and a scoundrel.

Now, her gaze darted from the musicians, to the silver bucket of champagne standing at attention beside the table, to the material-backed Parsons chairs tied with lavender bows. Dozens of small stone planters filled with red roses and tall pillar candles were set around the entire would-be dining room. She'd never gone into detail like this. She'd never mentioned to Alex the flagged stakes in the ground. Or the exact layout to the country house he'd promised to build her after they were married.

She'd never mentioned lavender bows or ivy and gardenias or roses.

She was sure of it.

Her mind swam, fishing for answers. Then, *bingo!* Her heart slammed against her chest. She shuddered, and Alex stepped up beside her, so close that his presence reassured her. If that wasn't the oddest thing, that he could still lend her comfort. Giving her head half a turn, she faced him and whispered, "You remember?"

He nodded. "I remember."

Her eyes squeezed shut. How many times had she prayed for his memory to return? "When?"

"Just recently."

"So you remember lying to me? Using me?"

His voice gruff, he laced his fingers with hers and gave her hand a gentle shake. "Cara, I remember loving you."

She melted a little, finally hearing the words she'd hoped to hear for so long. How many nights had she clasped her hands and lifted her head to heaven, praying that Alex would regain his memory? "I—I'm glad for you, Alex."

"There are only two things that matter to me, Cara. And your love is one of them."

She dropped her hand and distanced herself. He was too close. And he remembered. Oh, God. "You went to all this trouble to prove to me that your memory has returned?"

"Yes. I went to all this trouble. I wanted to remind you how much we loved each other."

The corner of her mouth lifted out of sadness. "Once, I loved you."

"Twice, I've loved you, Cara. Once, I loved you as Alex Santiago. Yes, that's true. But when I was injured, you came to me in the hospital and tried so hard to help me. I began to fall in love all over again. When I returned to my home, a place I didn't remember, you showed me what love is, what we'd had, and I fell in love with you again as Alex del Toro."

"Alex, please," she said. She didn't want to rehash this. She didn't want to remember the good times, the love. She especially didn't want to remember the night she'd seduced him, trying her hardest to get him to remember her. She'd gone all out, using every single erotic move and gesture she knew turned him on, to *turn on* his memory. It hadn't worked. Even after that night, Alex still hadn't remembered her. "What do you want from me?"

"I brought you here hoping that you'd hear me out. Hoping that you'd listen to what I have to say. I want you to understand what happened. I want to apologize for everything I've done to cause you pain."

Alarms clanged in her head. Did he really still love her? Or was his work for his father not through yet? Did he have more damage to do? How could he ask her to forgive him? She still bled from the pain and humiliation he'd caused. Anyone who picked up a newspaper or watched the nightly news knew of the scandal. The headlines might as well have read Cara Windsor—Idiot for Love. "I don't know if I can accept your apology, Alex."

The hopeful gleam in his eyes dimmed. He sighed and even that sound came out melodic. "Just listen to me before you decide. Will you have dinner with me?"

"Here?"

He nodded. "Here."

Her eyes narrowed. "You promised to have me back in an hour."

He didn't hesitate. "I'll honor that promise. I'll take you back right now if you insist."

Insist. Insist. But Cara's darn mouth was stuck in neutral. Nothing came out.

"Please, Cara. I have things to say that I haven't told another soul. You may not trust me, but I trust you. I need to explain everything to you."

She deserved an explanation. And he had her curious now. What kind of excuses could make up for breaking her heart and destroying their love? "Send the musicians away. There'll be no serenading and dancing tonight."

His breath rushed out. "So, you'll stay?"

"Only for dinner. I'll hear you out and then you'll take me back home."

A beam of hope entered his eyes. He nodded. "I promise."

A promise from Alex del Toro?

Maybe someone had some swampland in Florida to sell her, too.

Cara's eyes closed as she took her first bite of shrimp scampi. The shrimp and the linguini were perfectly cooked. Garlic and olive oil made everything better. The evening was perfect, right down to the best pairing of wine to accompany the meal and the pink-gold blaze of light setting over the river.

Leave it to Alex to make it all so memorable…even the second time around. But there wouldn't be any offering of engagement rings or talk of happily-ever-afters tonight.

"It's delicious," she said.

She waited for Alex to say something pertinent. He had explaining to do. But instead, his gaze flowed over her like warm honey, shifting from her hair to her mouth. Cara squirmed in her chair, aware of his eyes on her. If only she hadn't agreed to come here with him.

Was he remembering the last time they'd made love? Was he remembering how she'd seduced him, practically in his sickbed, the day after he was released from hospital? Fools in love do stupid things. She'd actually thought getting naked with him in his home would rocket from his groin to his brain and he'd remember her.

She closed her eyes and banished the memory.

"What is it, Cara?"

"Nothing." Everything. "Alex, you brought me here to explain. I haven't heard any explaining yet."

He set his wineglass down. "Where should I begin?"

"You lied to everyone in Maverick County. That's a start."

He began nodding. "Okay, okay. You're right. It all started with my father."

"The king of Del Toro Oil."

"Yes, he's the president and owner. He built his company from the ground up. When we were children, he worked long hours and there were days my sister and I never saw him. He's a man who wanted greatness, but he always wanted to protect his family. When Gabriella and I were kids, my mother…my m-mother was kidnapped as a result of his huge success and wealth. She was held for ransom. It all went badly and she was killed."

"Oh, no! I'm so sorry." How awful. Her heart ached for the little boy who'd lost his mother in such a violent way. "How old were you when it happened?"

"Eight, and Gabriella was just four."

As harsh as it was, it only cemented her feelings about Alex. A fiancée should've known about her future husband's hardships as a child. She should've known about his family, but Alex had hidden his past from her. He wasn't the man she'd fallen in love with. She didn't know this Alex at all.

"My father was obviously distraught over my mother's death. After that incident, he hired bodyguards for my sister and me. We went nowhere without protection. Mexico City can be a dangerous place, especially if you're the child of a wealthy, powerful man. Finally, when I was older and working exclusively for Del Toro Oil, I convinced my father to let me keep an apartment in Mexico City. I always felt like I was being watched, though my father would deny it. Then one day, he approached me about his plan to gather information about Windsor Energy. I would live in Maverick County and become an entirely different person. To come to America and pose as Alex Santiago, a business tycoon. I saw it as an adventure and my chance to rid myself of the danger in Mexico and finally be free. No one here in the U.S. would know I was Alejandro del Toro, Rodrigo's son.

"To my father, loyalty is everything. He was giving me this chance to prove myself in his eyes. He was pleased when I agreed."

"And over two years ago, you came and settled here."

"Yes, I became Alex Santiago."

"You ingratiated yourself into West Texas society. You were embraced by your neighbors. You were invited to join the Texas Cattleman's Club."

"I made friends, yes. Good friends. I made money here, on my own, and then…then I met you, Cara. And everything changed."

Her heart wanted to hear what he had to say, but her brain scolded her for listening.

"How? How did it change? You knew I worked for my father. I'm the director of marketing for Windsor. The only change that I could see is that I gave you the outlet to find out more information. You dated me for months and pretended to care about me."

It was love at first sight. She'd never believed it possible, but the moment she'd laid eyes on this tall, brown and handsome man—the second she heard the deep, rich timbre of his voice at a function at the Texas Cattleman's Club—Cara was done for. She'd been seeing Chance McDaniel at the time, and she broke it off instantly to be with Alex.

"I do care about you. I always have. When I met you, yes, I'll admit I thought it would make my task easier to get close to you. But if you think back and remember, I didn't ask anything of you, my love. I never questioned you about the company."

"You didn't have to. I was pretty good at coughing up information. I'd tell you all about my day, the ups and downs. How the company was faring against our competition and what I was doing about it. I'd tell you my strategies for marketing and get your opinion."

Bile rose in her throat. She hated that she'd been so naive with him. She hated that she'd been played for a sucker. Rehashing it all put a sour taste in her mouth. She pushed her plate away, fighting the burn behind her eyes. Her pride kept her tears well hidden. Crying was the last thing she wanted to do in front of Alex. His betrayal crushed her like a tiny ant under his Italian loafers.

"I can't make up for the past, for the decisions I've made. But Cara, once I realized how important you were to me, I was through with the charade. Right after we were engaged, I'd planned on convincing my father not to go after Windsor Energy."

Her shoulders stiffened. "Am I really supposed to believe that?"

"Yes, you are. Because the truth comes straight from my heart."

Cara glanced away, over the candlelight and past the roses, out into the dusky night sky. Gurgling waters lapping over jutting rocks filled the silence. It was so peaceful here. At any other time, she'd be happy to be here. This was her favorite spot on earth.

"Cara, look at me."

Her gaze shifted to his face. Alex by candlelight was something to see. Her life could've been so perfect.

"Soon after we got engaged, I was driving home late one night. I had a surprise for you waiting at my house. It had just been delivered and I was going to pick it up and bring it to you."

She swallowed. Under the table, her hand went to her tummy.

"But I never made it to your house. While I was driving I noticed someone tailgating me. I drove faster to lose him. But he sped up, too, and continued to hug my tail. From what I could tell, there were three big men in the car. The next thing I know, they're pulling up beside me and ramming my car. I was jolted from the sideswipe and realized these guys meant business. My car skidded off the road. I hung on to the steering wheel and tried to maneuver the car back onto the highway, but the driver never let up. Their SUV swiped my car again, staying neck and neck with me, until finally I couldn't outmaneuver them. I remember the crash. My car almost hit a tree and then I went spiraling down an embankment. The air bag deployed and protected me. A second later, I was yanked out of the car and beaten until I passed out."

The scene played out in her mind. She didn't need to hear all the details to know it must've been horrendous for him. "Alex?"

He began nodding. "It's all true, Cara. I must've been drugged, because when I woke up I was in an abandoned house. There was nothing around, no furniture, no food. I was groggy and disoriented, but I remember the stench of that place as if it was yesterday. I didn't know exactly where I was, but I knew I wasn't in America. My attackers left me there. I don't know if they planned on coming back to kill me or not, but I wasn't going to stick around to find out. I couldn't figure out why I'd been abducted but it seemed as though somebody paid them to rough me up and get me out of town."

Cara let that information sink in. Nothing was as it

seemed with Alex, but he'd gone through a horrible ordeal. She believed that much. He wasn't that good an actor. Something in his eyes spoke of genuine fear. "This is all so bizarre, Alex. You could have been killed."

He nodded. "I didn't know who to trust. I got out of there pronto. I found out I was in Tijuana. I used my gold watch to buy my way on a truck smuggling immigrant workers into the U.S. They packed a bunch of us inside and I tried my best to blend in with them. I'm Mexican, after all. I didn't look like a millionaire, and though some workers eyed me with suspicion, I kept my head down and pretended not to notice."

"You took a big chance with your life."

"I had no choice. I had to get outta there."

The truck Alex had been traveling in was sideswiped by a car and had careened onto its side. A dozen migrant workers had spilled out onto the road, Alex included. She'd heard it was an awful scene and there was a lot of confusion. A paramedic who'd showed up at the wreck recognized Alex, which was a good thing because the blows to his head during the accident stole his memory.

Alex took a few bites of his food while Cara sat silently, picturing what he'd gone through and wondering about this man who at one point she'd thought she'd known so well.

"When you left town, people started speculating about your disappearance. Chance was suspected of having something to do with it. I left him for you. Dropped him like a hot potato, and some believed Chance was insanely jealous. I never believed that for a second, but it looked suspicious to those who knew us."

"Chance's name needs to be cleared. I plan to get to the bottom of it. Chance is in love with my sister and they deserve a clean start. Someone had me shanghaied and I'm going to find out who it was."

Cara sighed as her guard came down a little. She never wished Alex any harm. She still didn't, but his abduction had little to do with her. It didn't make up for the fact that he'd betrayed her. "After all you've told me, it's a miracle that you made it home in one piece."

"I almost didn't. It was a stroke of luck that Piper was the paramedic on the scene and recognized me. I didn't know who she was. Hell, I didn't know who *anyone* was, but I'm grateful that she took charge and made sure I got the medical care I needed."

"And now you know who you are. So what's next?"

"I try to make amends with everyone I hurt. I try to pick up the pieces."

A waiter in tuxedo tails and white gloves took their plates away. Another waiter came by to scrape crumbs off the table and replace the cutlery.

"I want to move past this, Cara."

Easy for him to say.

"I'm asking only one thing from you."

Coffee was poured from a silver pot and domed dessert dishes were placed on the table, one for her, one for Alex. On Alex's nod, the waiter walked away, leaving them alone. Cara didn't want dessert. She didn't want to be here with Alex. Memories rushed in and carved out another slice of her heart.

Alex leaned over the table to pick up the dome and reveal her dessert. Her eyes lowered to a square wedge of rich chocolate brownie garnished with fresh whole raspberry mounds.

My favorite.

This time white frosting written on the dessert didn't ask, Marry Me? like before. But at this point in her life, the question scribed on the brownie meant almost as much: Another Chance?

Her lips quivered. She put her head down.

Alex reached over the table to take her hand, and the melting force of his warmth wasn't something she could fend off right now. "Before you say anything, remember how much we loved each other. Remember the happiness. And laughter. Cara, do you remember how we celebrated our engagement after I put the ring on your finger?"

Cara's lips lifted as her gaze shifted toward the river. How could she forget? It was one of those memories that would stay with her until her days on earth were numbered. It was a memory she wouldn't share with another soul. A snapshot moment she would always cherish.

With moonlight guiding them and hands entwined, they'd christened the quiet waters with their naked bodies, diving into the river and coming up with big grins, the heat of their love cloaking them from frigid temperatures. They'd splashed around, silly with joy, and laughed until their bellies ached.

"I remember," Cara said, her voice sounding whimsical to her ears. "It was the best."

"Yes, it was."

Their eyes locked and they stared at each other. But Cara wasn't going to be a fool again. Sweet memories only made the loss of their love harder to bear. It only reminded her of what could have been if Alex hadn't been deceitful. His little plan had backfired. She couldn't eat the brownie or stay here another second. She wasn't in the mood for decadence. She wasn't in the mood for forgiveness. Cara released his hand and shook her head. "I'm sorry, Alex. I can't give you what you want tonight."

His mouth puckered as he nodded. "I understand."

Do you really? She doubted he knew how much pain he'd caused.

"Will you take me home now?"

"Of course."

He rounded the table and pulled out her chair. As she stood, he took her hand. Steady on her feet, she looked into his eyes. They could be cold at times, like when Alex was determined to close a big deal, and she'd always wondered about his drive and determination. Now she knew exactly where those traits had come from. He was his father's son. Any man who'd send his only son to another country to assume a false persona and spy on a rival had to be ruthless. But in Alex's eyes tonight, she found only warmth and apology. He wasn't happy with her decision to leave so early, but true to his promise, he agreed to take her home.

Kudos to Alex.

She'd give him that much. But the one thing she wouldn't give him, the one thing she wasn't ready to share with him, could very well change everything between them.

Cara carried his child.

Two

Cara entered her cottage on Windsor Farms and tossed her purse down on the sofa. Her hand touched her stomach reflectively. Turmoil wasn't good for the baby. And she'd certainly had that today with Alex showing up at her office. Was it seeing Alex and hearing about his kidnapping that churned inside her? Or was it a case of morning sickness hitting her in the evening? She didn't know. She'd never been pregnant before.

How could she label the queasiness that gripped her stomach?

The history on her computer screen would alert anyone checking that she'd been boning up on symptoms of pregnancy. Only a short while ago she'd discovered she was carrying Alex's child and since then, she'd kept her eyes and ears open to anyone who mentioned "baby."

Leaning against the top of the sofa with one hand, she spread her fingers wide across her belly with the other.

According to her cell phone app, the baby was the size of a strawberry. That put a smile on her face. Imagine that? Protective instincts kicked in for her little strawberry and her tummy gushed with warmth. She'd do anything to keep her child safe, including keeping him away from his father until she was certain she knew what kind of man Alex del Toro really was.

Right now, she hadn't a clue. His touch still did things to her. He wasn't a man she could easily forget. She sent a quick glance heavenward. "Thank you," she remarked to the love gods. Alex hadn't tried to kiss her tonight.

"Darn him," she mumbled. Had she secretly wanted him to kiss her?

She exited the living room and strode down the hallway that led to her bedroom. As she passed her workout room, she shook her head. "Nuh-uh." Her limbs felt like Jell-O. She didn't have the energy for her regular stair-climb program. She continued down the hall, passing the guest bathroom, certain now that her tummy was beginning to settle and she wouldn't be making a quick trip to the toilet to purge her meal.

She reached her bedroom and wiggled off her heels, slipped out of her blazer, blouse and then unzipped her skirt and shimmied out of it. She pulled on a comfy gray sweat suit she'd lived in since her college days at USC, then barefooted her way to the kitchen. She hadn't had much to eat today. Period. *What to Expect When You're Expecting* didn't have to tell her the baby needed nourishment.

She knew she needed to eat, but the problem of her Alex-or-baby-induced queasiness was the issue.

She clicked on the light and blinked against the brightness. White cabinets and stainless-steel appliances wowed her. Her state-of-the-art kitchen kicked culinary butt and put a glow into her heart. She'd had the place overhauled to fit her lifestyle. Her four-bedroom cottage on the hills of her father's land at Windsor Farms had gone from country to contemporary after an extensive overhaul.

She loved walking in here. Almost as much as she loved comfort food, but sweet-potato fries, mac and cheese or double-nut chocolate ice cream weren't on her agenda today. She was in baby mode and didn't mind the sacrifice.

Opening her fridge, she pulled out a bowl of fresh-cut berries. She dumped them into her Cuisinart along with a banana, added two dollops of plain yogurt and a few ice cubes, then pushed the puree button. She got an earful of grinding noise and then the machine purred while whipping it all together. Voilà, the perfect smoothie was born. She poured herself a tall glass and took a big swallow. Icy chills raced straight up to her brain. "Oh."

Once her brain thawed, she took another sip and actually tasted it this time. Delicious! And just what the doctor ordered. There was no rebellion from her tummy, no nausea. A quiet hum coursed through her body. She'd done a good job of mothering tonight. Baby came first. She could get used to smoothies for dinner.

She brought the smoothie with her as she walked into the living room and plopped down on the sofa. Under her, cushions of chocolate leather creaked with newness. Aside from the updated kitchen, the living room was her second-favorite place in the cottage. She closed her eyes and guzzled down the rest of her smoothie.

Briiing, briiing. She had the only cell phone in the world that rang with an ordinary ring. She didn't want to think about what that said about her. Reaching into her purse, she grabbed her phone and answered on the second ring. "Hello."

"Hi, Cara. It's me, Gabriella. I hope you don't mind me calling this late."

"Hi, Gabriella. I don't mind at all. I'm up." Cara stared blankly at the remnants of her fruit smoothie riding up the sides of the glass sitting on the cocktail table.

"That's good. Are…are you alone?"

There was so much hope in her voice, Cara hated shooting Alex's sister down. "Yes. I'm alone."

"Oh," she said. Then there was silence on the other end.

Had Alex told Gabriella about his plans to hijack her from the office today? "Alex still doesn't know about the baby. I didn't tell him."

"I, uh, I understand. Alex said he had something special planned for you tonight, but that's all I could get out of him."

"I'm sorry, Gabriella. I know he's your brother and that you're concerned about him, but I can't tell him about the baby right now."

"Cara, I—I want you to know I'm not pressuring you. I'm very excited about my niece or nephew and, well, I'm so happy now. More than I ever thought possible. I'm so deeply in love with Chance that I want to see everyone happy, especially you and my brother."

"Oh, Gabriella, I wish things were different, but the facts will never change. You know how complicated it is between Alex and me. What he did to me, the way he betrayed me…"

Gabriella's voice lowered to a whisper. "It's unforgivable. *Sí,* I know. If it wasn't for the innocent child you carry, I would understand if you never forgave him. But he's my brother. And you're my friend. With the baby on the way…it should be a happy time for both of you."

"You're a good sister, Gabriella. And a good friend to me."

Gabriella's friendship was important to Cara, and they were becoming closer each day. Though no two people could've started out any rockier. Gabriella had walked in on Cara crying on Chance's shoulder when she'd found out she was pregnant with Alex's child. Cara had thought herself the biggest fool for sleeping with him right after he was released from the hospital and right before his true identity was revealed to the world. Twice she'd been fooled.

Gabriella found Cara in Chance's comforting arms and assumed the rancher she'd come to love was playing with her heart. She'd run off and Chance had to do some fast talking to convince Gabriella he wasn't still in love with Cara.

Only Gabriella and Chance knew about her pregnancy.

"That means a great deal to me, Cara. I want so much for us to be good friends and I thank you for your trust in me."

Trust she didn't dare give to Gabriella's brother. "I know you had no part in the deception. You explained it all to me."

"*Sí*. I am angry with my papa. He kept me in the dark about Alejandro. He never told me my brother lived under an assumed name. He never told me what my brother planned to do, only that business took him away from Mexico." Gabriella's voice trembled. "Alejandro almost died, though. It is hard for me to stay angry with my brother."

Cara saw her point. "We can be friends, Gabriella. We won't let Alex come between us. If you forgive him, it won't change our friendship. I am grateful to have you to talk to now that you are with Chance."

"My papa is not happy I have moved into Chance's home. He feels like he has lost control. And he worries. I have been sheltered most of my life, but now I have grown up. I have a good man. I will not let him go."

"Chance is a good man. And he's lucky to have you, Gabriella. I wasn't the right woman for Chance, but you are."

"He had nothing to do with Alejandro's kidnapping."

Cara pictured Gabriella as a four-year old child growing up without her mother. How sad for her. How devastating for the whole family to lose a woman they all loved to murdering kidnappers. She understood why Gabriella couldn't stay angry with her brother. Learning of his disappearance had to rekindle horrible memories for her. "I'd bet my life on it. Chance isn't made that way."

Gabriella's sigh of relief carried over the phone line. "I'm glad you believe it."

"Will you promise to keep my secret a little longer, Gabriella? I know it's asking a lot of you, but…I'm not ready to—"

"I understand. When I lost faith in Chance, I didn't know where to turn or what to do. Time will help you decide. We will keep your secret. Chance and I… We will not betray you."

That made her the only del Toro who wouldn't. Cara didn't hold Gabriella's bloodlines against her though.

"And remember, I am here, whenever you need me."

"Thank you, Gabriella."

The conversation ended, and Cara clicked off her phone. Tonight, Alex had revealed to her that he'd regained most of his memory and, on the drive home, he'd asked for her promise to keep it a secret. If he believed it would help him clear Chance's name and find out who'd had him kidnapped, Cara wasn't going to stand in his way.

It was one more secret to keep.

A quiet sigh blew from her lips. If only she'd fallen head over heels in love with Chance McDaniel. Life with him was easier. He was a good, honest, simple man.

Unfortunately, only Alex del Toro put butterflies in her stomach. Among other things. It was getting crowded in there. Butterflies and babies.

Cara laid her hand over her plank-board belly where a little strawberry grew.

And a teeny-weeny smile emerged.

"You know, your sister is a much better rider than you are," Chance McDaniel said over his shoulder.

Alex nudged his horse, and the mare caught up to Chance's mount as they traveled the McDaniel land, far into the hills. "That's because while she was out learning French and English and taking riding lessons on our land with only the best horsemen in all of Mexico, I was busy learning the family business."

Chance lowered the brim of his hat to the morning sun. "Yeah, well, look where that got you. Cara is barely speaking to you. You're in hot water at the Cattleman's Club and you're still not sure if the people who kidnapped you are planning a second course with you on their menu."

Dios! Chance was right. And Alex hated to stand corrected. Alex adjusted his black Stetson on his head and blew out a sigh. "There's nothing better than having a morning ride with my friend to clear my head. *Gracias,* McDaniel. You are overly kind."

A smirk spread wide across Chance's face. "I've been told that before. By your sister."

Alex laughed. "She's the kind one. My sister has a heart of gold. If you ask me, you got damn lucky the day Gabriella came into your life. And if you ever forget that…"

Chance gave a slow nod of his head. The right side of his mouth cocked. "Nope, never gonna forget that. Your little sis gave me a run for my money. If she'd made it all the way back to Mexico, I would've tracked her down and brought her home, where she belongs. I know what I'm getting with that woman."

Alex believed him. Chance was crazy about Gabriella.

And his little sis loved Chance enough to defy their father. In some ways, Gabriella had been smarter and stronger than he'd been. Pleasing bullheaded, powerful and ruthless Rodrigo del Toro had become an obsession for Alex. He'd wanted to make his father proud. To prove himself worthy of taking over Del Toro Oil one day. Coming to America, posing as Alex Santiago and living the life he'd always wanted was too big a temptation to refuse. Alex hadn't thought too much about the repercussions of that decision. He hadn't thought about hurting the friends he'd made here. And he certainly hadn't thought he'd fall in love with the daughter of his rival, the heir to the very company Del Toro Oil hoped to buy out.

Alex swiveled his head from one end of the range to the other. Rolling hills covered with budding wildflowers and prairie grass lay across the land. No one was in sight. "Listen, Chance. I asked to ride out here with you for two reasons. I think you know what I'm going to say, but let's get out of the sun."

"Fine by me."

Alex pulled up on his reins and his mare halted under a mesquite tree. He dismounted first and ground tethered his palomino. Chance did the same. Under the umbrella of long outreaching branches, checkered light filtered down and partially blocked the sunlight. The two of them sat down on a blanket of coarse grass. Alex leaned back against the tree and yanked a blade of grass from its root as he stared out onto McDaniel land.

"I've told you before, I will clear your name of any wrongdoing in my kidnapping."

"Crock of crap as it is."

"I never thought it was you. Not your style."

"What in hell does that mean?"

His face cracked into a small smile. "You'd try to punch

my lights out in a fistfight. You'd challenge me to a duel. You'd kick my ass if you thought you had cause. You're no coward. You'd face me head-on. Only a coward would have me run off the road and shanghaied, left to rot in a Mexican town."

"Glad you have such a high opinion of me."

"You and me, we'll be family soon. I hope our friendship is strong enough to survive this."

"I'm hoping so, too. Didn't much like it when Cara fell in love with you. I thought she and I had a future together. We fit. We came from the same background. But I stepped aside so that she could be happy. And look how you've hurt her."

Alex drew a deep breath. "I know. Believe me, I'm trying to make up for that. But it's trickier than you might imagine. For the past few weeks, since my memory has returned, I keep rehashing the details. I've got people poking around behind the scenes, trying to tie it all together, trying to figure out the mystery. And only one name keeps cropping up. It all makes sense. It's the only person with something to gain by having me kidnapped. I think Paul Windsor got wind of my real identity. He never liked me. He never wanted me with Cara. After we got engaged, I think he hired those thugs to come after me. They roughed me up and dumped me across the border."

"You think he figured out who you were? Didn't want to see his daughter tangled up with you and decided to get rid of you?"

Alex began nodding his head. "Yeah. I'm almost certain it was him."

"You got any proof?"

"Some. But what I do have is motive. If he knew what I was up to with Windsor Energy and that I planned on marrying his daughter—"

"He'd want you out of the picture."

"That's right."

"Okay, let me know if I can help with that. Even though Cara's old man never gave me any trouble when we were dating, if he's guilty of this crime he needs to be off the streets. It's hard thinking anyone in the club could do something this criminal. I guess you never know about people."

Alex nodded.

Chance looked him up and down, with warmth vacant from his eyes. "Of course, you had me fooled, too. You succeeded in deceiving me and everyone who called themselves your friend. Once, I thought you could do no wrong."

Alex tossed the blade of grass down. A breeze picked it up and it landed ten feet away. His eyes homed in on the sliver of grass and his mouth quirked. If only he could do that, get from point A to point B that quickly. He knew where he wanted to be, back in everyone's good graces. He'd had the world by the tail and he'd let it slip through his fingers. He might never live down what he'd done. His gaze slid to Chance sitting right next to him. He'd been his best friend. And how did he repay him? By stealing his girl and lying to him. Alex was lucky Chance gave him the time of day.

"I hope I can make it up to you. I've been thinking, since my father is still in Texas and will be staying at my house until Gabriella is properly wed, what if I gave you a wedding? Gabriella can have the wedding she has always wanted, big or small. I know you are itching to get hitched, as you say." Alex smiled. "It'd be my honor to do this for both of you."

Chance lowered his head. Apparently, he found the grass interesting as he stared, unblinking. Overhead, branches rustled in the wind and chirps from nearby crickets interrupted the silence. "Well, now," Chance said, lifting his lids and squaring their gazes. His voice rasped, "That'd be a darn good start at repairing the damage. I think Gabriella would love that."

Quiet breath released from Alex's chest. "I'll ask my sister today."

"That'll make her happy," Chance said.

"I hope more than Cara was." Sensations whirled in his gut. He still smarted from Cara's brisk dismissal of him last night. She wasn't cutting him any slack. At least he'd gotten a chance to tell her his feelings for her were stronger than ever. He wasn't going away. His stubborn streak ran a mile long. "She's not thrilled with me these days."

"If you love Cara and want her back, this thing with her father isn't going to help. You go after him, you stand to lose Cara, too. She'll be hurt by this."

Alex couldn't deny that. "What choice do I have?"

Chance shrugged. "None, I guess. You're right. It's tricky."

"I appreciate you hearing me out, Chance. I hope one day you'll fully welcome me into your family. Giving you a wedding is just the beginning."

Alex put out his hand.

Chance gave it a glance and then nodded. As they shook on it, Chance said, "If Gabriella wants this wedding, you've got yourself a deal."

He smiled.

It would be the best deal he'd made all year.

Gabriella could be dangerous with a rolling pin in her hands, but she'd forgiven him for the most part, so he ambled to the doorway of Chance's kitchen, eyeing his little sister working at the counter. Wearing an apron decorated with cherry-topped cupcakes in pink and white and chunky turquoise jewelry around her neck, she stood beside the range top, rolling floured dough into paper-plate-size circles. Steam rose from the griddle and she wiped at the beads of sweat on her face with her forearm, her long dark hair pulled back out of her eyes. She lifted her creations and dropped them onto the heat. They sizzled.

He leaned against the door frame and watched his sister's precise movements with amazement. She'd never been an adept cook. Living with Chance had changed his sister. "Tortillas like *Tía* Manuela used to make."

Gabriella turned sharply at the sound of his voice and blinked rapidly. "Alejandro?"

"I had business with Chance today. He let me into the house a minute ago."

"You remember *Tía* Manuela?"

"We would go there on Sundays after church. She'd make us a batch of warm tortillas and fill them with potatoes and beans. They were delicious and we'd always fight over the last one."

Gabriella's dark eyes grew round. "She would tell you to let me have the last one."

"And I would because I knew she would make up another batch just for me. I would then eat three more and *mi hermana* could not keep up with my appetite."

The memory was a good one. Alex smiled as his little sister's eyes watered. "Alejandro, I am happy your memory has returned." She turned off the burner and took a step toward him and embraced him. She'd only recently learned that his amnesia was gone.

He nodded. "*Yes.* I am haunted with memories of playing tricks on my sister and having the wrath of Papa come down on my head. As you know, I remember everything."

Alex was grateful most of his memories with his sister were good ones. He hadn't given her too much trouble while growing up. Except for normal harmless big-brother antics, Alex and Gabriella had a loving relationship. He, like his father, had been protective of her, and she didn't always appreciate being sheltered and overprotected. He recalled her rebellion when Papa had allowed Alex to move out of their secured mansion to live in an apartment in Mexico City...to become a man.

Gabriella had cut her long luxurious hair to a bob style that measured no more than three inches around her head and had a tattoo inked on her shoulder. By then a furious Rodrigo del Toro had had enough. Luckily, Gabriella's tattoo disappeared on its own after one week as she'd claimed. That single saving grace resulted in her not being punished. But she'd definitely made a statement. Alex had admired her guts in her temporary rebellion.

Gabriella pulled away from their embrace to take his face in her gentle hands and stare into his eyes. "I wish those awful things had not happened to my brother. Do you know any more about the ones who did you harm?"

He glanced away from her soul-searching eyes. "It is better not to discuss it. You do not need to know the details."

"I am not a child. I can handle the details. I'm concerned for my big brother," she said, studying his face. "I will not wilt away knowing the truth. Are you in danger now?"

"I'm cautious, Gabriella. But I feel the danger is over. I plan to find out who did this to me and do my best to put to rest any rumors that Chance had anything to do with my abduction."

For Gabriella's safety, Alex wasn't going to confide in her about his suspicions. The fewer people who knew his memory had returned, the better leverage he would have. "And you, my sister...you are no wilting flower. You have made me proud standing up to Papa. He has babied you long enough. You are in good hands with Chance. He will take care of you."

Her mouth opened instantly. "Alejandro!"

"Let me finish. Chance will see to your needs, I have no doubt, and you will take care of his. You will be equal partners. Is that not what marriage is all about?"

Her expression softened as she contemplated. "*Sí,* it's what I always believed marriage to be. Alejandro, please be careful."

Alex used his thumb to wipe a spilled tear off her cheek. "I will be. Until I find out who was responsible for the crimes, no one but family will know my memory has returned. I revealed my secret to Cara last night. She owns my heart, Gabriella, and I only hope she will one day forgive me, but she has promised not to tell anyone and I trust her."

"I will continue to keep your secret. You know you can count on me." Her smile was big and warm and shining with love. "Today is a happy day. I will focus on that. Will you stay for some of *Tía's* tortillas?"

"You don't have to ask twice. I wasn't leaving until I had me a bellyful."

She chuckled, her light, joyous laughter stirring memories of their childhood at Las Cruces, their family's estate. "Now you sound like Chance."

"And every other Texan in the county."

Gabriella's smile radiated through the kitchen, brightening his mood. She turned to the griddle as Alex stepped beside her. "I have another surprise for you."

"What could be a better surprise than your memory returning?"

"Well," Alex said, "I have a great deal of making up to do."

"Agreed." With spatula in hand, she flipped the tortillas over. "There are so many you have deceived."

The hairs on the back of his neck rose. Gabriella was a little too eager to agree with him. "And even though you were my tagalong little bra—" The spatula smacked his forearm. "Hey, that's hot!" Damn, his sister was quick.

She grinned. "You were saying, I was a—?"

"The best sister in the world?" He rubbed the sting from his forearm.

"Better," she said with a nod. She wielded the spatula his way and gestured for him to go on.

"I want to throw you a wedding, Gabriella." All joking aside, Alex couldn't think of anything he wanted more for his sister. "Before Papa returns to Mexico, you could speak your vows at my home in Pine Valley. I'd make sure you'd have the wedding of your dreams. Whatever you wanted, I would provide."

Slowly, Gabriella lowered the spatula. He eyed the thing and was glad his arm was out of danger now. Lifting his gaze to his sister again, he marveled as the sweetest expression stole over her face. Growing up, Gabriella had never been a problem to him. He simply loved to tease her, and now it was important to him that she allow him this honor. "Oh, Alejandro."

Tears of gratitude and love swam in her eyes and his heart warmed. "That is very kind of you. Chance and I want to be married quickly, but we have not made our plans yet. We want nothing big, but only to be married with our family and friends in attendance."

"Done."

"Are you certain?"

"I'm sure. Let me do this for you and Chance."

She began nodding. "*Gracias,* Alejandro. Thank you. Thank you. My heart is filled with happiness today."

"Mine is, too, *mi hermana*. You deserve it."

She smiled again and offered him a seat. "Let me finish cooking. I will give my big brother the entire batch of tortillas."

"With beans and potatoes?"

"*Sí.* It is your favorite."

Alex left Chance's house with a full belly. Why was it that food from the past always tasted better? Always satisfied more? Up until a short while ago, Alex didn't really know which foods were his favorites, which ones were held over from his childhood, which foods turned his stomach. Now all of it was back, and *Tía* Manuela's fresh warm tortillas had put a smile on his face as he gunned the engine of his SUV and drove down the path that led him off McDaniel's Acres. Before he reached the gate, his gaze hit upon a blonde woman entering the stables. His mind flashed, familiar and female, and his heart pumped hard against his chest.

Cara?

He braked suddenly and parked the car on the side of the road. Taking brisk steps, he entered the stables and squinted from lack of sunlight. Once his eyes adjusted, he scanned the aisles, searching for the woman he'd seen just seconds ago. Footprints marked the ground and hay rustled, but otherwise all was quiet. How far could she have gone?

Then movement caught his eye. Down along a row of stalls, all the way at the end, he found Cara with her arms folded on top of a stall door, her eyes fixed on a mare. Her hair was drawn back in a loose ponytail and secured with a rubber band. She wore white jeans and tennis shoes, obviously not riding gear, and a flimsy pale blue button-down blouse. The ball cap on her head screamed Dallas Cowboys in bold blue-and-silver lettering.

Alex couldn't keep from staring at her and strained to hear the soft, soothing words she granted the horse. Finally, his feet moved and he headed down the long aisle, catching the eye of Striker, the mare he'd taken out this morning with Chance. He clucked his mouth, and the horse's ears perked up. Cara stayed focused on the mare, even as his boots parted hay and crunched as he moved closer.

Without her knowledge, he took in every graceful move she made. Relished each uttered sweet word drifting to his ears. When he stood within five feet of her, she turned her head to one side and found his eyes. He was caught off guard by the softness on her face, the kindness in her expression. He'd expected anger or rebuke when she noticed him, but instead her lips lifted slightly.

Alex halted and caught his breath. His heartbeats fired rapidly. "Cara."

"Hello, Alex."

He drank in her blue depths and the mellow tone in her voice. *Dios,* how he loved her.

"What are you doing here?" he asked.

"Visiting my friend." Her gaze dropped over the stall to a bay mare. "I rescued her a few months ago and Chance lets me keep her here."

Alex moved closer to glance at the horse that had put Cara in a melancholy mood. The mare was average size, probably a mustang, marked with two white stockings on her front legs and a coat that was a little duller than the ones in Chance's well-cared-for string.

"I thought you were afraid of horses?"

"I'm getting over that. This horse has changed me. She's special."

"She must be to get you to come into the stables without blinking an eye. What's her name?"

"Mercy." She stared at the horse. "When I laid eyes on her that was the first thing out of my mouth. *Mercy.* She was abused and neglected. There were maggots living in her coat. They were eating her alive. I didn't think she'd survive. She was starved and jittery. It broke my heart to see an animal suffer that way."

"Terrible. How often do you come to visit?"

"As often as I can, but it's not always possible. Chance has been good about it. He gives me updates on her condition."

"She's going to survive."

"I think so. She's still nervous with people. She's got trust issues and I don't press it. As long as she's cared for, I'll wait until she's comfortable enough with me before I step inside her stall."

"That is probably wise. I'm sure she appreciates your visits. She will come around."

She shrugged and directed her gaze to the recovering horse. "It's not a hardship for me. I…I missed her today."

The hint of sweet vanilla teased his nose as Alex stepped closer to Cara. He inhaled deeply to savor her scent over the more potent musty barn smells of earth and straw. Images flashed in his mind like a flip book, one scene after another. Cara giving him cooking lessons. Cara just stepping out of the shower. Cara sprawled out across his bed, waiting for him. "I know something about missing someone you care about."

The slightest flicker in her eyes told him she'd heard his comment. "Cara, look at me."

Her eyes closed as if she was in silent prayer. A few seconds ticked by, and he used that time to move a step closer. His heart hammered hard as he waited. And finally she turned and opened her eyes. They fluttered like butterfly wings.

She wasn't as immune to him as he'd feared.

"Alex, what are you doing here?"

"I met with Chance earlier. We rode."

"I mean, what are you doing *here?*"

"I got lucky. I was pulling away after seeing Chance and my sister when I spotted you coming in here."

"Oh." She nibbled on her lip and looked away. No eye contact. He wondered if his candor broke through some of her defensive walls. "Did you follow me?"

They'd already wasted enough time, months, and he'd be damned if he let her slip through his fingers now because of his foolishness and her pride, so he told her the absolute truth. "I am not following you, if that's what you're asking." He couldn't blame her for wondering. Yesterday, he'd hijacked her from her office. Today was simply a blessed accident. "But as soon as I saw you, I followed you inside the stable."

Her eyes lifted to his.

He brought his hand to her face and touched her cheek gently with his fingertips. Breath puffed from her chest in a whispered sigh as she closed her eyes and absorbed his warmth, telling him what he wanted, needed to know, with unspoken words. "You haven't forgotten what it was like between us?"

Her head moved. "No."

"We had heat, Cara." He drew deep from the well of her sweet scent and brought his mouth to hers. His lips hovered over hers and he rasped, "We still do."

She kept shaking her head, but her eyes betrayed her. She still cared, she still loved him. No longer fierce and protective, those orbs of blue welcomed him with timid acceptance. He had to prove to her he wouldn't hurt her again. If she gave him another chance, he would show her pleasure and try his damnedest to make her happy.

"Alex." He took her plea as invitation and not rejection.

He thumbed her chin up and brought his mouth down. A squeaky noise erupted from her mouth as soon as their lips met and Alex smiled then, unable to hide his satisfaction. She was everything to him and he wanted to be everything to her. Again.

Her mouth was exquisite and he wanted more…already, so much more. He'd been too long without her, and the evidence wasn't too far south of his belt buckle.

He put his hands on her waist and drew her up against him. Her body fit him perfectly. She was snug against him as the kiss deepened. He nipped at her lower lip and she opened for him, her breaths as ragged and rapid as his own.

He swept through her luscious mouth and groaned as she met his demands. Licking her with his tongue, he tasted the sweetly heady combination of wholesome and sexy all rolled up into one. Cara had been forbidden fruit, the daughter of his rival, his best friend's girl, yet he hadn't been able to keep away from her. He couldn't now. Her taste permeated his core, giving him an erection that strained fiercely, killing him in small measures. His juices flowing hot and liquid, he splayed his hands around her backside and with a quick, gentle jerk, her hips collided with his. "This is our heat, Cara."

She answered with a low, aching moan rushing from her lips.

He let his hands roam over her jeans and cursed the damn sequined pockets barricading him from feeling more of her. He ached to touch bare skin, to feel her warmth and curve his hands over the twin swells of her cheeks. He broke contact with her mouth only long enough to take another ragged breath. "I remember you. What we had."

"Alex." She jerked her head back far enough to meet with his eyes. She gulped air, her eyes liquid clear and hungry. "We can't…"

He blocked out her refusal and grabbed her hand. Tugging her along, away from the stalls, away from any daylight, he found an empty office at the end of the barn that was no longer in use. He pulled her inside, noting an old pine desk and dusty papers covering a metal file cabinet. The door locked and the plastic blinds were already lowered on the indoor window.

She glanced at the desk, her brows arched in silent thrill. He was way beyond that, *thrill* too shallow a word for what he felt for her, but he could not take her on that filthy desk. He thought too much of her. She deserved more. He settled against the wall, and pulled her to him. She landed flat against his chest, her curvy body flush against him. He groaned at the perfect fit, the way she filled in the hollow spaces both of his needy body and his vacant heart. He'd blown it with her. There was no sugarcoating the obvious. He would make her remember the couple they'd once been one little gasp, one smoldering kiss, one fantastic orgasm at a time.

He cupped the back of her neck and jerked her head forward. Her mouth was a breath away. "You have no idea… what you do to me."

Cara started to make a quick retort—she was sharp with her tongue—but he was quicker. He crushed his mouth to hers, staking a claim that was long ago decided. She didn't pull away, didn't rebuke his bold move bringing her inside the abandoned office. She was torn, though, with indecision; he tasted it in her kiss, her slightly stiff body against his. He hoped to melt her, to make her see the truth about them.

Alex was not a patient man. But he'd wait for Cara as

long as it would take. But not before he left his mark on her. Not before he gave her a memory they would never forget.

His senses pulsed as he deepened the kiss and murmured soft, loving words. He broke through her rigidness, nuzzling her throat, his nose tickled by silky locks of her hair. He touched her shoulders and smoothed his hands down her arms. Her body responded with little tremors that he felt under his fingers. "You're so beautiful, Cara."

"So are you…. That's why this is so hard for me."

"I'm sorry for all I have done to you, sweetheart."

"Don't…say any more," she whispered. And in that whisper he knew she asked not for apologies that were hard to accept but for something more carnal. Something he'd planned to do for her anyway. "Let me make it up to you."

Already his hands were on her waist, his fingers nimble on the button of her jeans. He unfastened it and took the zipper in his thumb and forefinger. She didn't protest, didn't jerk away, but the tremors escalated and there was a twinge of movement toward him, enough encouragement for him to continue. He held her hip steady with one hand and inched down the teeth of her zipper with the other. Her jeans separated over her belly, and she splayed her legs open. For him. Alex dipped his hand inside her heat, brushing his thumb and pinkie finger against her firm, smooth thighs. Lacy material covered his destination, and he moved it away with a single finger slide.

She gasped, her body shaking now and arching toward him.

He touched a finger to her folds.

Sweat beaded his forehead, and other parts of his anatomy grew damp. His mind whirled and landed on thoughts of her coming to his bedside when he was still injured. Bringing her body to his, seducing him with soft words, pleas to help him remember her. She climbed him and took him inside her, trying to help, trying to rekindle what they'd had.

Today, he intended to do the same. To bring her pleasure, to ask for forgiveness, to give her the pleasure she so deserved and take nothing in return.

He brought another finger to join in, caressing her with applied but gentle pressure. "Ah...Cara. Tell me this doesn't feel right."

She whimpered and melted into him.

His lips sucked moisture from her mouth.

A low and guttural groan emerged from her throat. It was sweet to his ears.

When he touched her again, she jerked in response and sucked on his mouth, kissing him feverishly.

Heat.

"I haven't forgotten what you like, Cara, my love."

He opened his hand wide, separating her thighs more, and cupped her with his palm. Shallow breaths hissed from her lips, and he extended his hand, lifting the heart of his palm up, meeting with awaiting flesh that welcomed the intrusion. He palmed her up and down, and she gyrated in full sync to his cadence, the thrusts of his hand.

"Please, Alex..."

A look of lust and pent-up desire captured her expression as her plea ripped him to shreds. His blood pulsed like rapid fire through his veins. He'd almost forgotten his mission to bring her the greatest pleasure. With damp folds beckoning, he inserted his finger and found the most sensitive, heat-driven spot of her womanhood. His strokes meant more than mere sex—they were telling her with each glide, each tease, that he remembered how to please her. That he loved to pleasure her. That she meant the world to him.

Brazen cries broke through her softer sounds. It was

beautiful to see her react to him, to see her doubts subside, her hatred of him disappear. Today, right now, he was not a piranha but a man who cared deeply about her. A man who would sacrifice for her. A man who owed her so much more than this.

Yet, she was a beautiful woman, signaling him for more. He could hang clothes on his erection, with the way it stood now. He would never be named for sainthood and wasn't sure how much more he could take. The tantalizing scent of her sweat fragranced the air and it was time. He applied greater pressure to her soft wet folds. "Now, Cara."

The quakes started slowly, a building of frenetic energy that escalated with every bold caress. He summoned every bit of moisture from her pulsating body and whispered commands encouraging her limitlessly to rocket the release and give in to the intensity. "Take it, Cara. All of it," he rasped quickly and quietly into her ear.

In another second, she exploded around them both, her juices a firebrand to his hand and relief to his heart. Tension poured out of her like a balloon rapidly losing air, releasing pressure. After her spasms ended, he let her come down naturally, squeezing her tight with one arm, planting tiny kisses to her face while his hand remained at her womanhood, reluctant to leave until she was completely through.

He'd brought her to orgasm in less than a minute's time. It had always been that way with Cara and him. They ignited like dry wood to flame and burned brightest when they were together.

"Alex…" She sighed, cradling his cheeks in her hands. She kissed him lightly and then the bright wild flare in her eyes dimmed. It wasn't enough. He knew it wouldn't be. Cara hadn't just been injured by his betrayal; it was nearly a death blow to her.

"It was beautiful," he said, crooking up half his mouth. "And only for you."

This didn't change anything, she told him with a gleam of silent regret in her eyes. But then, a glimmer of light returned for a quick second, giving him a morsel of hope before she turned away.

With her back to him, she zippered her jeans and straightened her blouse and ponytail. He regretted not slipping that rubber band off and riding his hands through her honey-blond locks.

Alex composed himself, his manhood still inflated behind his trousers. If he couldn't have Cara, a cold shower would have to do.

She stared at the window to his side, her eyes narrowing and her face twisting up. "I don't know when I'll forgive you, Alex. I don't know *if* I can."

"I am impatient, Cara. I want us together now. But I will wait for you to decide. I will do just about anything for you."

Her gaze slipped below his waist. "Are you going to be okay?"

He shrugged and leaned back against the wall. Looking at her through heavy lids, he answered, "I will survive. Today was for you, Cara. But if you should ever want… need me, I will always be available to you."

Amusement invaded her eyes as she smiled. Her quick orgasm and this smile brought him hope. "For a booty call?"

"Dios." He pushed off the wall and stepped toward her. Her face still held the remnants of sexual satisfaction. Imagining her coming to him freely for late-night love-making didn't help his swollen manhood one bit. "I would not refuse you in any way. At any time."

Her sharp inhalation reached his ears when she nodded. "I'll remember that."

Alex wasn't keeping score, but he might have won this round today.

Distant voices drifted into the room, disturbing their privacy. Immediately, Alex took her hand and walked her to the back of the office near the file cabinet and away from any light that would reveal their silhouettes. He did so only for her protection. He didn't give a damn who saw what, thought what, when it came to Cara. But she would care. She would not want Chance's work crew seeing them coming out of the office together and getting the wrong impression.

Or in this case, the *right impression*.

Any embarrassment to her would land on his shoulders and he was already digging himself out of a foxhole with her.

"I think they're gone," he whispered, squeezing her hand.

Cara stared at the door. "I've got to get out of here." She pulled her hand free, and he wondered if she was relieved or sorry to go. From the tone of her voice, he couldn't tell. "I've got an early dinner date with my father. The last thing I need is for him to question me if I'm late."

"He should not have that much control over you, Cara."

Cara's shoulders stiffened, and she glanced away.

The last thing he wanted to do was make her angry right now.

"The same way you shouldn't have allowed your father to manipulate you into doing something deceitful?" Her gaze fell back on him now.

It hadn't taken much manipulation on Rodrigo's part. Alex had needed a change of scenery, a change of lifestyle and wanted to branch out on his own. He had not thought of the consequences of his actions, that much was true, and he'd wanted to prove his worth to his masterful business tycoon father. But to fall so hard for Windsor's beautiful daughter? He hadn't seen that coming. And the train wreck was not over yet. "You're right. I tried to please my father, the same way you try to please yours."

"He wanted a son, an heir for Windsor Energy and all he got was me. But I love him. We have a complicated relationship."

"Yes. The same is true with my father. Complicated. Powerful men usually are. But your father should be glad to have such a loving, loyal daughter. You're every bit as good as a son. He should know that."

If Alex could prove her father guilty of his abduction, he would have to hurt her all over again. He didn't entertain the thought very long. Cara was halfway to the door.

She unlocked the handle and put her hand on the knob.

"Cara?"

She turned, her watery blue eyes pleading with him to let her go. "I can't do this..."

He had more to tell her. More he wanted to share. But it hurt to see her in such pain. To see her nibble at her bruised lips with indecision. He wouldn't press her. Today was about pleasing her. "Go...I'll wait a few minutes before I leave."

She nodded. "Goodbye, Alex."

Her tone slashed him with finality.

It wasn't over. She should know that about him. He painted on a smile for her. "I will see you soon, sweetheart."

She walked out, and Alex's breath pushed out of his chest. He glanced down. It would be a few minutes more before he could exit the office. Cara was going to be his again. He didn't know how he would accomplish it, but it would happen. He was determined.

And that was one trait he'd inherited from his old man: he never gave up when he wanted something.

Three

Solid stone walls of the Texas Cattleman's Club gave him a friendlier greeting than some of the cold wooden faces staring at him as he entered the one-story building and made his way to a reserved private room. Judging eyes admonished him and gave him no reason to feel welcome. He hadn't been thrown out of the club. Not yet. And he would make sure that he wasn't. Amends took time and he had a plan in mind that would put smiles on the members' faces. He damn well hoped it wouldn't backfire.

The club was a place where he'd made friends, negotiated handshake deals until they could be ironed out by Legal, where he'd played hard and where he'd often keep open ears for any news about Windsor Energy.

He opened one of the double-paneled doors and let himself inside. Immediately, his gaze flew to the two men he'd asked here. They sat in bulky brown leather chairs, three tumblers of whiskey two inches high rested on a chunky black-walnut table. A large landscape of Texas plains, cattle and drovers hung over a massive stone fireplace.

The men rose as he entered, and he extended his hand to the sheriff of Royal first and then to the TCC president and owner of the Straight Arrow Ranch. "Nate, thanks for coming. Gil, same goes to you."

Bailey Collins, Gil's fiancée, was once assigned as the state's special investigator to solve his disappearance. When Alex returned to town, the case had been given lower priority and was turned over to local authorities and del Toro's private investigators.

The men sat down, and Alex took a seat on a comfortable sofa facing them. Leaning forward, bracing his elbows on his knees, he got right down to business. "I appreciate you being here, so I'm not going to waste your time. Or mine. I think I've got some proof about my kidnapping that you both need to know."

Nate and Gil exchanged glances.

"My memory is back, but I hope to keep that information confidential for now. I know I will have your full cooperation. I think it will be easier for me to gather the information and keep the suspect guessing that way." He gave each man a chance to agree, which they did with a nod. "I was beaten and abducted and taken across the border to Mexico. Let me give you a clearer picture of my life and the events leading up to me being taken."

Alex spent the next twenty minutes describing the details of his abduction to the men, starting off with the night he'd been run off the road. Nate encouraged him to be as specific as possible and Alex battled with his memory, trying to remember exact details.

When he was through, Nate gave a low whistle. "Well... now we know. It's good that your memory is back, Alex. I'm happy about that."

"I am, as well." Alex took a sip of smooth Jim Beam and let it slide down his throat.

Gil scrubbed his chin and studied him carefully. "And you're one hundred percent sure Paul Windsor is behind this?"

Alex stared at him and shook his head. "I can only be sure the sun will rise every morning, but I have enough evidence to put me at ninety-nine point nine percent."

"Those are lofty odds," Nate said. So far, he hadn't touched his whiskey. The sheriff must be on the clock. "What proof do you have?"

"Windsor never liked me as Alex Santiago."

"For good reason," Nate said, his hand coming up, palm out. "Just keeping it real, Alex. You were spying on his company."

"I did nothing illegal."

"You dated his daughter and he was suspicious of you from the beginning," Gil said. "There's no doubt now, he hates you for what you've done. He's come to me on three separate occasions urging me to make a motion to oust you from the club."

Alex inhaled a sharp breath. "I hope that won't happen. As for Cara, I was just about to tell her the truth, when I was kidnapped. I think Paul Windsor somehow figured out who I really was. I think he could not stand it when Cara and I got engaged, and he wanted me out of the picture. Maybe permanently."

"So, you said you had evidence," Nate said. "What is it?"

"My father has many connections in Mexico, as you might imagine. After my mother was kidnapped and killed, my father went to great lengths to see to our family's safety. All through the years, he's had eyes and ears out in all of Mexico. Right now, he's got people working on my behalf to find out who is responsible for what happened to me. His reach is far longer than mine. So we're checking out two sources right now.

"One, the house I was dumped into in Tijuana can be traced to Windsor indirectly. There's a paper trail he probably figured would never be discovered tucked under one of his subsidiary companies. The house was once used for employees for a company Windsor owned years ago."

"It's a stretch. There's no way to prove he'd known about the house," Nate said. "Circumstantial at best."

"There's more," Alex said. "My father's contact spoke to a bartender at a local watering hole in Tijuana. The bartender claimed there is a man who comes in regularly when he is in town. This guy has a girlfriend who lives at the border. Anyway, the man is a real boozer and he was spending money left and right on one particular night. He whispered something in the bartender's ear, boasting about how he'd made a load of dough for running someone off the road and dragging his sorry butt to Tijuana. The contact gave us a name. The man lives in a small town south of here."

"A name? Now how did he get that?"

"The bartender was persuaded to give it up for a price." Alex said. "Money talks and so does the del Toro name."

Nate gave in and took a sip of whiskey. "Give me the name of this guy and the info you have on the location and I'll run it down."

"Done."

"There's no guarantee that this man will pan out," Nate said. "Don't get your hopes up."

"And no way to know if the story is true. Could all be a coincidence or nothing at all," Gil added. "But my instincts tell me Windsor might be behind it."

"He has motive," Nate said.

"I think he is guilty." He didn't want him to be, for Cara's sake, but Alex's instincts were leading him in Windsor's direction. "For a time there, when I was just coming to in that house, I didn't know if I was going to be killed or not." Alex paused, a chill gripping him. "I got the hell out as fast as I could. If Windsor was behind the kidnapping and beating, then he's a very dangerous man."

"I agree. He needs to be reined in if he's guilty. Mind if I run this by Bailey?" Gil asked. "Since she was in on the original investigation, she might be able to help."

"I don't mind," Alex said. Bailey Collins had trained with the FBI. "She's a smart woman."

"The smartest. She ended up with me and Cade, didn't she?"

"When you're right, there is no way to deny it." Alex pictured little four-year-old Cade Addison in Bailey's loving arms, being a mother to the deserving little boy. "Give Bailey my best."

"Will do."

"Okay," Nate said, rising from his seat. "Get me that info as soon as possible and, in the meantime, watch your back, del Toro."

"I plan to." His father insisted on extra security at Alex's office and his home. He had agreed it was necessary. But there was no way he would walk around with a bodyguard dogging him. He'd had enough of that when he was a boy. Alex knew to be on guard now and to trust no one.

Nate began walking to the door. "Thanks again, Nate." They shook hands. "I'll be in touch." Alex opened the door for him and turned to Gil, who was putting his hat on.

"Gil, if you have another minute, I want to run something by you," He offered him his tumbler. "You can finish your drink while we talk."

Gil's brows rose, and he gripped the brim of his hat,

tugging it off. "Uh, sure. What is it?" He swallowed a gulp and stared at the remaining whiskey in his glass.

Neither of them chose to sit again.

Alex lifted his tumbler and gave the contents a swirl. "What would you say if I developed and funded a college scholarship for the employees' children here at TCC?"

Gil paused, sending him a serious stare. "Really?"

"Yes. I've been thinking of a way to make up for all the chaos I've caused. I want to show everyone who I really am."

"You want to buy your way out of trouble with the other members?" The side of Gil's mouth crooked up.

"That's a harsh way of saying it."

"That's what everyone will think."

"Regardless of what they think, the bottom line is I would be helping kids less fortunate than I was. That is what's most important."

"You've got a point there. Wouldn't hurt your tarnished image, either. I'm all for mending fences, but there's always gonna be some who will not be happy about this."

Alex didn't know if he would ever regain the trust he'd abused of the friends he'd made here. "My intention is to prove that I have changed and to make amends. I plan to name the scholarship after my mother. She was one who believed in higher education. She would approve of my idea."

Softness entered Gil's eyes. He knew the whole story about Elena del Toro.

Alex had been a young boy when his mother was kidnapped and murdered. A memory flashed of the day he'd been told his mother would not be coming home, and his throat thickened.

"Well, now, I'd have to bring it up for a vote," Gil said. "I like the idea. Should've happened years ago. You're making it hard for the members to vote this down. It's either a yes vote, or they'll look bad in the employees' eyes. And we all know they have a gossip grapevine that runs a mile long."

"True, the odds are stacked in my favor, but that's not the real reason I'm doing this."

Gil's lips slipped into a smug smile. "You're a smart one, del Toro. You've made it so everyone benefits from your plan."

He grinned. "I hope so. I may have been a renegade, but I'm a Texan now."

Gil laughed. "You might just be that. Okay, work up your proposal for the scholarship and get back to me. If all looks well, we'll put it to a vote."

"*Gracias,* Addison."

"*Da nada,* Alejandro."

After his meeting with Gil and Nate, Alex stepped into the arched double-door entry of his Pine Valley house. Instantly, he was struck by the bright interior as sunlight filed into vaulted ceilings that gave an illusion of greater space to his already spacious mansion on the golf course. His steps echoed on the ornate stone foyer that opened in three directions to rooms for dining, entertaining and relaxing, depending on the pivot of his heels. The interior was furnished with exquisite taste by a decorator he'd commissioned when he'd bought the place, and the exterior's best asset, aside from an oversize black bottom waterfall pool and lush grounds, was the absolute privacy the place provided.

Now, the house that was meant to allude to his persona and success as Alex Santiago wasn't that any longer. The house he'd taken for granted when he'd started the charade wasn't merely a vehicle to uphold his fake image.

It was home.

"Is that you, Alejandro?" His father's distant voice carried from the kitchen. Even a simple question, when spoken from Rodrigo del Toro's lips sounded like a rebuke.

"I'm home, Papa." Alex closed his eyes. He wasn't in the mood to spar with his father tonight.

His pivot took him toward the kitchen and onto the patio. He found his father seated on a lounge chair, feet up, with a tall pilsner glass in his hand. He sipped Mexican beer and gazed out at the grounds. "The duck pond is overflowing today."

End-of-day light streamed onto the water, and ducks took off and landed like a busy day at Dallas Fort Worth Airport. Still, his father's tone suggested sarcasm, whereas Alex enjoyed the view, ducks and all, after a long day at work, so he ignored the comment.

He took a seat beside his father on a padded wicker chair. "I've told the sheriff and TCC president our suspicions. Nate will investigate Windsor from his side and we will have our answer soon."

Rodrigo's smooth brown face bunched, making him look every bit of his fifty-five years. His eyes darkened to an inky glint as he snapped, "I do not trust anyone but my own men to see justice done. Windsor will pay if he was the man responsible for your abduction."

"Papa, we are not in Mexico any longer. We've discussed this already. Your men gather the information, and then we turn it over to the law. It has to be this way."

An almost imperceptible nod was the only assurance he gave Alex. Not a good sign, but the best he was going to get from his mulish father. "I don't want any action taken unless we know for sure that Paul Windsor gave the orders to have me taken. Cara… She will be hurt by this. I can't have that on my head, Papa. Cara is too important to me."

"She will not speak to you. She will not have anything to do with you."

Yesterday, he might have agreed with that, but what happened in the McDaniel's stable today changed things. He gave Cara reason to believe that what they had wasn't easily thrown away. She was like a blooming flower in his arms, opening to him by the sun of hope, but also petal delicate and completely vulnerable to his touch.

How many times lately had he dreamed of holding Cara that way and making her come apart in his arms? How many times had he prayed for another chance with her? "That's not exactly true. I saw her today after I visited with Gabriella. I hope to repair the damage I've caused her."

His father shrugged, keeping his focus on the pond where a mama duck ushered five baby ducklings out of the water. Alex would smile at that scene, if the man before him wasn't trying his patience.

"Why bother with her? She is the daughter of our enemy. She is—"

Alex hardened his voice with conviction. "The woman I want."

"Her father is ruthless. A murderer."

"We don't know that for sure." Although Alex did not think he was wrong about the perpetrator of his abduction, he wasn't sure murder was Windsor's intent. "I am here, alive and well, taking breaths on my own."

His father whirled on him, his eyes fierce. "By. The. Grace. Of. God. *Dios,* Alejandro, you were missing for a long time…an eternity for a father who did not know what was happening to his son. You cannot begin to know my heartache. Or that of your sister."

Maybe Alex didn't know the full extent of his heartache. Rodrigo prided himself on his children's safety, especially after what had happened to his wife, Elena. His father had never forgiven himself for not fully protecting her and bore the guilt of her death on his shoulders.

"I cannot change what happened." *To my mother or to me.* When his father had heard of Alex's accident and amnesia, he'd gathered up Gabriella and come to America to help Alex regain his memory. By doing so, he'd told the world that Alex Santiago was a fraud. Unintentionally, as his father was frightened for him, Rodrigo had practically openly confessed to his plan to undermine and possibly buy out Windsor Energy. He'd acted out of love for his son, but the consequences of his actions had backfired on Alex. Especially with Cara. "I will be more careful now, Papa. I know Windsor is a dangerous man, but we must proceed slowly to catch him."

"He will not get away with endangering my son's life." His father had a choke hold on the half-empty glass he held. Any second, Alex expected to see the glass shatter.

"No, he will not get away," Alex said quietly, "if he is guilty."

His father drained his beer and stood, imposing his breadth and height over him. Only a light gleam in the depths of his eyes told Alex of his father's affection for him. "Your housekeeper, Maria, has made meat-filled empanadas and rice. They are not as good as your mother's, but I am hungry. We will have dinner."

"*Sí,* Papa. I'll shower and change and then I'll tell you my plans for Gabriella."

"What of your sister, Alejandro?"

"We'll discuss her marriage to Chance. I am throwing them a wedding here."

His father's eyes bore through him. "Another lost cause. A lot of good Joaquin did. The bodyguard did not do his job with Gabriella."

"I'd say Joaquin excelled at his job. Gabriella found love

and has never been happier." Score one for his sister. "Is that not what you want, Papa? Your children's happiness?"

Rodrigo blinked, pondering a question that should be answered easily by a parent. "Exactly. *Si*. I want Gabriella happy, but not with the gringo. He is not the man for her."

"Papa, she thinks he is. And she's not going to change her mind. You can accept it or lose Gabriella forever."

Rodrigo's eyebrows rose and a look of astonishment stole over his expression. Alex didn't care. His father had to face facts. His children had grown up. They made their own decisions now. Good or bad, he couldn't dictate their lives any longer.

Alex turned away. Score one for him, too. Gabriella wasn't the only one to make Rodrigo del Toro see the light.

Her fingers strummed the tabletop, tap, tap, tapping as Cara waited for her afternoon date. The Royal Diner was known for their decadent chocolate cream and fruit pies. Normally the two didn't go hand in hand, but at Royal, they knew how to mix the cocoa confection with berries to make a winning combination. Usually, Cara didn't indulge, but today she could almost taste it on her lips. *Today,* she craved chocolate.

Since when had she caved in to her cravings anyway?

Her mind instantly jumped as she pictured Alex satisfying another of her cravings. Yesterday, she'd craved *him* and he hadn't disappointed her. His smooth baritone voice had stirred lusty memories, the dark penetrating fire in his eyes had scorched her skin and a single well-placed touch of his hand had sent her entire body soaring. If she kept running into him, it wouldn't be long before she melted entirely into a mass of forgiveness. She wasn't ready for that. Maybe in time she'd find a way to forgive him, but she wouldn't forget what he'd done to her. Right now the pain was too fresh, too raw.

Her heart was still broken.

Last night, after rehashing, and secretly reliving, their meeting in the stables, she'd come to the conclusion that the best way to protect herself from further injury was to keep her distance from him. If she didn't see Alex, her wounds would heal in time and she could move on.

Her gaze shifted to the diner's window-glass doors. Where was Gabriella anyway? She was late and Cara's chocolate craving was going into overdrive.

She'd waved off the coffeepot-bearing waitress two minutes ago. Babies and caffeine didn't mix.

Now the waitress was back with a tall glass of orange juice. "Here we go." She set it down on the table in front of her.

"Thank you."

"Would you like to see the menu now or wait for your friend?"

"I'm here, I'm here." Gabriella's heels rapped against the checkerboard floor tiles as she climbed into the booth, slinging her purse down. "Sorry I'm late, Cara," she said, offering a smile.

"Oh, it's no problem." Gabriella's dark hair, pulled back into a tight knot, added to her Latin beauty. Cara didn't know too many women who could get away with wearing such a severe hairstyle. But Gabriella rocked it. Her features were exquisitely sharp, with skin offering a natural sheer glow. Her smile was sweet and friendly. To think, at one time, Gabriella was jealous of her. Thank goodness that was all behind them now. Gabriella was the right woman for Chance. And they deserved a happy ending. "Is anything wrong?"

"Not at all. Chance and I were in a meeting with my

brother this morning and I lost track of time. Alejandro is being wonder—"

Cara's heart nosedived into her stomach.

"Oh, Cara…I'm sorry. Does it upset you if I speak of my brother?"

Yes. Yes. Yes. I am not over him yet. "No, it's fine. Of course you can speak of your brother." Cara glanced at the waitress, who stood patiently by.

She didn't miss her cue. Dressed in a fire-engine-red uniform and a stark white apron, the waitress stuck a menu under their noses. "Welcome to Royal's," she said mostly to Gabriella. "Now that you're both here, shall I give you a few minutes to decide?"

"That's perfect," Cara said with a smile. "Thank you."

As the waitress walked off, Cara asked, "What were you saying about your brother?"

She owed Gabriella her loyalty and friendship, since she was taking a leap by keeping Cara's secret from Alex. Cara put aside her own heartache to listen to what Gabriella had to say about her brother.

Brightness entered Gabriella's eyes and her mouth curved into the biggest smile. "Oh, Cara. Alejandro has offered to give me a wedding in his home. Is that not wonderful?"

"It's very kind of him," she said, doing a mental happy dance for Gabriella and Chance. How could she not be thrilled for them? They deserved a happily-ever-after. She had to give Alex credit for making his sister happy.

"Chance and I discussed having a small wedding in the judge's chambers. We wanted to be married quickly, and Chance knows that I am a traditional woman at heart. I am living with Chance as his fiancée, but nothing would make me happier than to be his wife. He wanted that, too, as soon as we could have arranged it. And now, Alejandro will host our wedding. It is the best gift of all to have my brother and father attend my wedding. Even though Papa is against the marriage and does not think Chance is worthy of me, Alejandro has been helping me convince him to attend our ceremony."

"I know it means a lot to you." It wasn't easy hearing news of Rodrigo del Toro, since he was the designer of Alex's little plan to spy on Windsor Energy. But he was also Gabriella's father and she loved him, flaws and all. Cara had to remember that. "Will you take your vows before a clergyman?"

"*Sí,* there is a deacon from the church who will marry us. The three of us met with him today. That is why I was late."

The waitress returned with notepad and pen in hand. Gabriella's eyes were still gleaming as she ordered coffee and lemon raspberry pie, though it wasn't the thought of pie keeping the perpetual glow on her face.

"Good choice," the waitress said. "It's my personal favorite."

The waitress glanced at Cara next. She waited for an ounce of guilt while ordering Royal's most sinful specialty and was relieved when desire won out over good sense.

Alone again, she found Gabriella's eyes on her. "You are Chance's good friend, Cara." Her softly spoken words flowed with the rhythmic beat of her Mexican heritage. "And now, you are my good friend, too. I feel closer to no other woman in Texas and I would like to ask you if…if you would be my maid of honor. W-would you consider standing by my side while I speak my vows to Chance?"

Goodness. She hadn't expected this.

Gabriella watched her carefully, her soft brown eyes warm and filled with hope. The affection between them had grown surprisingly strong as their budding friendship developed in a short span of time. She'd come to really love Gabriella del Toro as a dear friend. "It would be my honor, Gabriella. I would love to be your maid of honor."

Gabriella rose slightly, coming halfway over the booth with arms outstretched, and Cara met her in the middle. Their embrace was awkward and loving and then both giggled happily before returning to their seats.

"I'm very glad to have you for my friend, Cara."

"I feel the same way. I've never been a maid of honor before, so you're going to have to steer me in the right direction."

"And I've never been a bride before. We'll, how do you say, muddle through together?"

"Yes, that's how you say it. It'll be an adventure."

Though Cara's plan to keep her distance from Alex was shot to hell before she had a moment to implement it, she reasoned she couldn't very well avoid Chance and Gabriella's wedding day or deny her friend her request. Cara's heart tugged at the notion of being included in her friends' wedding. She wouldn't miss seeing them marry… not for the world.

"There's so much to do before the wedding." Gabriella paused, as if this was the first she'd really thought about it. "I need a dress and shoes and a guest list! *Dios.* I don't know where to start."

Cara reached over and clasped Gabriella's hand. "Don't worry about a thing. I will help you with everything. You will be a beautiful bride."

Gabriella's shoulders immediately relaxed. "*Gracias.* I had always envisioned being married in Mama's wedding gown. But there is no time to make the arrangements. The wedding is in one week."

One week? Wow. Even for a small gathering, that was speedy. The faux-leather seat cushioned her as she leaned back. "Let me help you find the perfect dress. I know a bridal shop that will bend over backward to accommodate a new bride. They have the most gorgeous gowns. Everything will come together, I promise you." She mustered enough reassurance in her tone to convince both Gabriella and herself.

Gabriella blew out a breath of relief. "*Gracias.* You have made me feel better about my wedding already."

Cara glanced away as pangs of heartbreak struck her chest. She, too, should be planning a wedding. She'd had the details set in her mind, what designer she would use for her dress, the perfect bridal bouquet, her favorite flowers adorning the tables. It was all a distant memory now yet the pain lingered, clinging on with heart-gripping force that refused to let go.

She turned back to Gabriella, giving her a smile, and realized it was too late. Her friend saw the misery she had momentarily forgotten to hide. "Cara…this is selfish of me. You have not gotten over—"

"Nonsense, Gabriella. This has nothing to do with Alex and me. I want to do this for you and Chance."

Joy blossomed on Gabriella's face again. "If you are certain."

"As sure as the sun sets in the west."

Gabriella's eyes narrowed in question. "It is an American expression?"

Cara nodded. "It means I'm one hundred percent sure."

When their dessert was delivered, Gabriella's eyes rounded at the size of the piece on her plate. "I cannot eat all of this."

Cara had no such high hopes for her own piece of pie. She was eating for two. "Take half home to Chance. He'll love it."

"I will do that."

Cara dug into the whipped cream first. A jolt of sugary sweetness burst into her mouth. "Yum. I haven't lost my sweet tooth. I should feel more guilt about this." A forkful of berries and chocolate cream entered her mouth next, and she sighed. "But I don't. It's delicious." She patted her stomach, and Gabriella's thoughtful gaze fell to her belly.

"Is the baby doing well?"

"Yes, I think so. I see the doctor next week again."

"Will you find out then if it's a boy or girl?"

She shook her head. She'd gotten her hands on every baby book she could find and read about private companies that could detect the sex of the child at eleven weeks, but Cara would wait for the real deal. Medical professionals got an accurate picture at nineteen weeks. "I won't know for a little while longer."

Gabriella leaned forward, her curious eyes glistening. "I am very anxious to find out. If it's a girl, I will make her a set of jewelry like no other. I have ideas in mind already."

"If she takes after me, she'll love all forms of baubles. And if it's a boy?"

Gabriella's face twisted and a guttural groan replaced her normally sweet tone. "Oh, well, if it's a boy, he will have an empire to…"

Cara's throat constricted at the thought of her son inheriting del Toro Oil. Her head clouded up and she couldn't utter a word. Up until this point, with Alex in the dark about her pregnancy, she didn't have to face the realities of what a son might mean to both families. Her throat wasn't working, but her stomach made up for the lack of bodily functions. It churned like a grinder spewing sourness on the sweet sensations rippling through from the pie.

Gabriella's hand flew to her mouth. "*Dios,* Cara. I'm sorry."

"It's not your fault." She shrugged, releasing stiffness

in her own shoulders. "I can't think of the future right now. I'm dealing with the situation one day at a time. The best thing for me to do is to focus on helping you have the wedding of your dreams." She drew a deep breath to fill her lungs, clear her cobwebs and steady her. "And that's exactly what I'm going to do. So see, you're helping me. There's no reason for you to be sorry."

Gabriella immediately lowered her lids and shook her head. Cara sensed she didn't fully buy into her bravado. "In the future, I will think before I speak."

"You didn't say anything wrong." Gabriella lifted her lashes to Cara's smile. "It's me. I'm the one with my head in the sand." And because she didn't know if Gabriella knew that expression, she said, "It means that I'm not facing my problems head-on. I'm hiding out. Because I honestly don't know what else to do right now. Trust me when I tell you, helping you plan your wedding is going to be more fun than I've had in months."

"Really?"

"Yes. Now, why don't we start by tackling that guest list…"

Four

Neatly groomed columns of lavender bluebells, white daffodils and pink zinnias parted the pathway Cara strolled as she made her way toward the cottage. The flowers in full springtime bloom never failed to lift her spirits after a day of hard work. Setting her purse and laptop down on the living-room sofa, she headed for the bedroom.

Eating for two had its rewards. She'd pigged out today at the Royal Diner and didn't regret a second of it until she was behind the wheel of her car and halfway home. Her stomach rebelled from abuse for a few minutes, reminding her that guilty pleasures needed some balance. Lucky for her, the revolt was over and Cara was back to her sensible-eating self.

She opened her bedroom door and glided inside. Her gaze immediately hit upon a legal-size note written with a Sharpie that she'd left on her bed this morning.

Dinner with Dad tonight.

She grumbled and let out a moan. "Oh, man."

She'd forgotten. All day long she'd looked forward to spending a peaceful night at home. After her over-the-top dessert today, she planned on having only a bowl of Cheerios for dinner. Her dad wouldn't let her get away with taking a rain check. Melanie was coming over tonight and heaven forbid if Cara should slight the woman that might become the fifth Mrs. Paul Windsor.

Thank goodness her mother wasn't around to see the debacle he'd made of his love life after she'd died.

Cara spilled out of her clothes, tossing each piece into a heap on her bed and giving the note she'd so efficiently written this morning a slow but complete burial. Too bad the damage was already done. No Cheerios for her tonight.

Naked now, she laid a hand over her belly. Every day she took measure and every day her plank-board belly answered in return. No baby bump yet. As much as she wanted to see the baby thrive and grow inside her, she relished the secrecy even more. It gave her time to sort things out in her mind and come up with a game plan. Playing Monopoly with her life wasn't fun, but it was necessary. She'd landed on Chance and didn't have a clue where the flip of the card would take her. One thing she knew for sure, Alex wasn't getting a Get Out of Jail Free card.

She grinned at that and took an almost endless shower that prickled her skin and rejuvenated her body. She'd need the fortification for the upcoming "Paul and Melanie Show." After the shower from heaven, Cara donned a sleeveless turquoise dress dotted with tiny white flowers. She wrapped a matching belt around her waist and slipped into a pair of white flip-flops decorated with pearls and a perfectly shaped carnation flower.

She let her hair dry loose. It was stick straight and thick enough to look groomed even if she did nothing but run a comb through it. She'd won Best Hair in high school but always wished she'd won Most Likely to Succeed. Being Paul Windsor's daughter, her friends always thought she had it made, but she'd never taken her job for granted. She worked hard to earn her title as marketing director.

She was halfway to the living room when her doorbell dinged. Furrowing her brows, she headed toward the front door, giving a glance at the wall clock on her way. Only seven? Was her father being impatient? Dinner wasn't until eight o'clock.

She pulled the handle and swung the door wide open. Her eyes lit on Alex, standing on the doorstep wearing expertly tailored black trousers belted in black leather with a white silk shirt tucked into his waist. The combination of black against white was breathtaking. Relaxed casual looked like a million bucks on him.

He stood at an angle, as if he was inspecting the grounds, and then she was hit with the force of his beauty as he turned to fully face her. "Hello, Cara." A quick white smile flashed against bronzed skin.

Cara blinked. She didn't think he'd have the nerve to show up anywhere near Windsor property after what he'd done. Then again, this was Alex, the indomitable man who'd marched into Windsor Energy the other day to kidnap her. "Alex. I'm, uh, surprised to see you here. H-how did you get onto the property?"

Her home, nestled one mile into Windsor Farms, also had its own private entrance with a security gate off the main road. It gave her the independence she needed and allowed her guests to come and go without having to disturb the security personnel at Windsor Farms. But the cottage also afforded her the convenience of living near her childhood home.

"I remembered the gate code," he said without apology.

Cara winced and immediately put changing the code on her list of priorities for tomorrow. She couldn't have Alex showing up on her doorstep anytime he wanted.

"You called me today. Twice," he said.

"Yes, I did. But I just asked that you call me back. I didn't expect for you to…" Her eyes lifted to his hair, shining like cool onyx against the fading sunlight. "For you to come over."

"You said it was important."

"Yes, well…I think it's important," she stuttered. His presence turned her world upside down. Darn him. She should send him away, but she really needed to speak to him. Her gaze locked on him like a homing device. Unable to look away, she pictured him in the McDaniel's stables, touching her, making her come apart in his arms. Instantly, a hot blast of heat climbed up from her belly to parch her throat.

"May I come in?" His smile and the softly spoken request charmed her.

"Oh, yes. Come inside." She stepped back and made room for him to enter.

He strode inside and turned around a few feet away. His presence and the sexy scent of his familiar cologne surrounded her. "You look beautiful, Cara."

So did he. It was par for the course with Alex. He devastated. "Thank you."

"Are you going somewhere tonight?" He probed her casually but with underlying intensity in his gaze. Was he jealous? Did he think she'd date another man? She still wasn't through the wreckage of their relationship. "Just dinner with my father and his latest lady friend."

He gave a nod.

Finally, good manners set in. "Would you like to sit down?"

"Yes, I would," he rasped. Why was it every word he spoke to her sounded like raw sex?

She waved toward the sofa. "Have a seat. I don't have a lot of time, so I'll make this quick."

"Okay." He sat in the middle of the sofa, which gave her the option of sitting next to him on either side. She took a seat in a chair facing him, but she had to give him points for trying. "The place looks good. I've missed coming here."

If he remembered everything, he'd know they christened the sofa half a dozen times, making love.

His hand splayed out and he stroked the fabric on the cushions.

Yeah, he remembered. She took a big swallow and forced her mind to the reason for her phone call. "I understand that you are throwing a wedding for Gabriella and Chance. I think it's very nice of you."

"I love my sister and am happy to do it for her."

His quick admission rippled through her. A man who loved his sister couldn't be all bad. Then again, Gabriella was pretty darn lovable. "And Chance?"

"He's good with it, too. We've talked and he's on the path to forgive me. One day soon, we'll be family."

With Alex's charm and good deeds he'd be granted forgiveness by everyone he'd deceived at the Cattleman's Club, too. It was just a matter of time. But his betrayal to her was the greatest one of all and she wasn't about to surrender her heart so easily again. "Gabriella's asked for my help with the wedding and I want to surprise her with something. But I need your assistance. Do you know exactly where your mother's wedding dress is stored?"

Obviously somewhat surprised at the question, Alex lifted his eyes toward the ceiling, thinking. He blinked a few times then answered, "I would guess it's with the rest of my mother's things at Las Cruces. My father had her possessions stored in a locked room on the estate."

"Will you ask him and then get back to me? Gabriella's fondest wish is to be married in her mother's gown, but she fears there's not enough time to have it located and sent. I say there is. What do you think?"

"My father won't be too happy about the request. But don't worry, I'll find a way to locate the dress. If it's still at the house, we will rush it here."

Every woman should have the wedding of their dreams. Yes, Gabriella would make do with a store-bought wedding dress. The most important thing was that she would marry the man who held her heart, but Cara saw Gabriella's sad expression and the regret in her eyes when she spoke of her mother's wedding gown. "It would be an amazing surprise for her. Please don't mention it to her. Right now, she believes that we're going dress shopping. And we will. I'll make sure we have a backup dress for her, just in case, but as soon as you tell me the dress is in good shape and on its way, I'll have a seamstress ready to do any last-minute adjustments."

"Cara…that's…that's a gesture my sister would treasure forever." Alex eyed her with admiration. "I will help in any way."

"We can only try."

"I have only seen the dress in wedding photos. My father keeps one by his bedside at home, and I can understand why Gabriella would want to wear it."

"Do you think your father…" Oh, how she disliked speaking of the man who wanted to destroy her father's company. "Do you think it would be too painful for him to see Gabriella in the dress?"

Alex tilted his head to the side, thoughtful. "It may be difficult for him, yes, but he loves my sister. If Gabriella wants to marry a gringo in my mother's dress, it will be done. I'll make sure my father cooperates."

Cara's shoulders stiffened. "Thank you. Could you also make sure your father doesn't destroy Windsor Energy while you're asking?"

Alex's lips thinned and he sighed. "I have made my position clear to him, Cara. I have explained to you that after our engagement I planned to confront my father and demand that he stop all proceedings to take over the company."

Cara wished she could believe the sincerity in his eyes and the resolve of his words. If only she had faith in Alex.

They sat facing each other as moments ticked by.

"Cara…" Alex's rich voice settled over her. It was the same erotic tone he used to bend her to his will when they made love. It was the same deep penetrating voice he'd used while coaxing her into a mind-blowing orgasm the other day.

"Don't, Alex."

He nodded and lifted up from his seat. Her gaze rose along with him as he unfolded his body to stand to his full height. He moved like a cat, full of sleek grace and pinpoint agility. "I will let you know what I find out from my father."

Cara rose also, a little surprised and maybe disappointed that Alex gave up so easily. Was she a piece of work, getting what she'd asked only to want more from him? Was she that unsure of her feelings that she needed to know he wasn't giving up, though she had no intention of giving in?

"I'll walk you out," she said.

Sidling up next to him, she meant to lead the way, but his hand slipped over hers, and he entwined their fingers. Her traitorous heart jumped from the thrill of his touch.

She should've known he wouldn't give up that easily. Part of her rejoiced, because losing a man like Alex del Toro wasn't a claim to fame. Just the opposite.

He drew her close and, as she lifted her face to his, their gazes locked. He smiled with his eyes and squeezed her hand gently. His gaze pierced something softer and more vulnerable inside her. Then one hand reached out to cup her chin and nudge it higher. He used the pad of his thumb to draw the outline of her mouth. It was the barest of touches and before she knew what was happening, Alex's lips were on hers, giving her perhaps the sweetest kiss she'd ever received. He left an indelible mark on her when he pulled away, leaving her wanting more. "Don't give up on me, Cara."

His beautiful deep brown eyes bore into her. "You don't have to say anything. Just know that I'm here, wanting you. Whenever you are ready."

She swallowed then gave him a nod.

"I'll be in touch."

"T-thank you."

After she closed the door, she wondered if she was thanking him for the kiss or for helping her out with Gabriella's wedding dress.

She rested her head against the door and sighed.

She honestly didn't know.

Cara pushed food around on her plate. They were having Melanie McNamara's favorite meal, Irish stew. She was sure her father's chef had gotten it right.... Paul Windsor paid attention to detail when it came to courting his women, but Cara didn't find the food appetizing or appealing.

"Are you not feeling well tonight?" Melanie asked.

Melanie wasn't a bad person. Actually, of all the women

her father had been involved with over the years, Melanie might just be the nicest. She was fortyish and had Sharon Osbourne–red hair and kind amber eyes.

Paul reached over to take Melanie's hand. "She'll be just fine."

Cara nibbled on her lip, shifting her gaze away. Her father's reassurance was for Melanie's benefit.

"Will you be?" Melanie asked, glancing at her with skepticism.

Cara's approval rating of her went up a notch. She was sensitive to Cara's mood and seemed to truly care about her. Of course, that also might have had something to do with the fact that Melanie was a marriage and family counselor. That's how her father hooked up with her in the first place. She'd counseled Dad with wife number three. It couldn't be called a conflict of interest or deemed unsavory, according to her father, because he'd had one marriage in between and didn't ask Melanie out until that fourth marriage ended.

"If there's anything you'd like to talk about, woman to woman, I'd be happy to listen. We could have a private talk," Melanie said.

Psychoanalysis was not on her agenda tonight, thank you very much. Although Melanie's concern seemed genuine, Cara was certain her father had filled Melanie in on the details of her pitiful love life. Everyone in Maverick County knew something about the Santiago/Del Toro situation. Alex's amnesia story had been all over the local news. The del Toro family made a big splash when they did something, and now most people knew about Alex's betrayal and their breakup.

Cara didn't want pity, though her father didn't exactly churn that out by the handful. Instead, he'd waved a dozen or so I-told-you-so fingers at her.

"Thank you. That's very sweet of you," Cara said to Melanie. "But I'm okay. I'm just not very hungry tonight."

"But you will stay for dessert? We're having crème brûlée," her father said.

After the rich dessert she'd had with Gabriella at lunch, she wasn't going to subject her stomach to more sugar. It wasn't good for the baby. So far, morning sickness hadn't hit, and she didn't want to tempt fate. She'd been lucky having no symptoms other than slight queasiness and sensitive breasts. All normal, she'd read, for a pregnant woman. "No dessert for me, Dad. But I'll stay for a cup of tea."

His mouth curved into a satisfied smile. "Attagirl."

Cara returned his smile. Her dad could be a good father when he wasn't talking business or looking over her shoulder at the work she did for the company. Often, she wondered if he would've rather had a son, a true heir to Windsor Energy who'd dive headfirst into the family business. Her father had never actually said that to her, but Cara always had a sinking suspicion deep down in her bones that her gender put her at a disadvantage. Telling him that she'd conceived Alex del Toro's baby would not only send his blood pressure off the planet, it would be validation to his belief that having a son would've served him better.

After the dessert was served, Cara rose and excused herself, giving Melanie a quick embrace. Her father graciously walked her to the door. "You are okay, aren't you, Cara?"

"Yes, I'm fine. Eager to climb into bed."

He sighed and flashed concerned eyes. "You'd think you were the middle-aged one."

"Maybe you're the one who should act his age, Dad."

"What? You don't like Melanie? She's smart and—"

"She's great and I do like her. But my opinion has never mattered to you, Dad. You've never asked me about the women in your life. You just barreled into one marriage after another. But maybe this time you should get to know her a little better before jumping into a serious relation ship."

Her father's face reddened, a clear sign Cara had overstepped his goodwill. "You're one to lecture me about relationships. Look at what happened with you and del Toro. That man was a real snake charmer and fooled you good. I won't forget how much he hurt you, nearly destroying my company in the process."

It hurt hearing her dad put her in the same category with his company. Paul Windsor lived and breathed Windsor Energy, and Cara often wondered, of the two, which one mattered most to him. This was not a conversation Cara wanted to have tonight. Hindsight was twenty-twenty. She should've zipped her lips and said good-night rather than get into a sparring match with her dad. "I know you're never going to forgive me for bringing Alex into the picture, Dad."

He shook his head. "That's nonsense, Cara. I've never blamed you for that. I hate that del Toro broke your heart. I never liked him from the beginning and had my suspicions about him. You know I always have your best interests at heart." He glanced toward the dining room and sighed. "I've got to get back to Melanie. Let's not argue," he said in a softer voice. The tiny blood veins that had colored his face were no longer visible. Controlled and dapper, Paul Windsor was back in true form. He placed a little peck on her cheek. "Sleep well, button. I love you."

The chill in Cara's heart warmed a little. She had to face facts—her father would never change. He was as inflexible as granite on affairs of business and a man with an eye for the ladies, but he did love her. "I love you, too, Dad."

Cara left her father's house and drove to her cottage. Once inside, she flopped down on the sofa, leaned her head against the back cushion and closed her eyes. The baby was sapping her energy lately. She needed more rest. Fatigue was typical in the first trimester, and Cara wasn't going to wear herself out. She'd already had Gayle cut half of her social obligations for the next few months and she was hiring another assistant. No more twelve-hour work-days for her.

She'd gotten away with making those changes without anyone questioning her motives. They all believed it was because she needed time to nurse her broken heart.

Cara's cell rang and she made a face. She let it keep on ringing, hoping that whoever was on the other end would hang up so she could go to sleep. Voice mail could do its job at ten-thirty in the evening. By the fourth ring, Cara's curiosity got the better of her and she dived into her hand-bag, plucking up the phone. Alex's face popped up on her screen. An intense wave of love swept through her and caught her completely off guard. Then she remembered Alex wasn't her fiancé anymore, and those precious few moments were lost to her. She spoke a little too gruffly into the phone. "Hello, Alex."

"Cara...what's wrong?"

"Nothing's wrong, I'm fine," she said sharply.

"It doesn't sound that way to me." The smooth, under-standing tone in his voice soothed her nerves. "Oh, baby, did you have another argument with your father tonight?"

Tears she blamed on hormones welled in her eyes. Once upon a time, Cara trusted Alex and shared some of the dis-agreements she'd had with her dad while growing up. And lately, there were many things they didn't see eye to eye on, especially her former relationship with Alex Santiago. That ranked highest on the list. "We didn't argue. I had dinner with him and his girlfriend, but I wasn't very hungry. I was just getting ready to turn in when you called."

"Sorry if I disturbed you, but it's good to hear your voice."

It was good to hear his voice, too.

Where was all of her blustering pain and anger when she needed it the most? Alex shouldn't be able to release endorphins in her body anymore, yet an invasion of warm fuzzies began circulating.

"I have some news about the wedding dress."

Cara raised her head from the sofa, hinging forward. "Good news, I hope."

"Very good news. I put in a call to our housekeeper at Las Cruces and she knew exactly where the dress was located. I gave her permission to unwrap the box and look the dress over. She was always close to Gabriella and was happy to help her. She said the gown is in very good condition. After my mother died, my father had it cleaned and preserved. It'll be here the day after tomorrow. I'm having it sent directly to you, if that's all right."

"Yes, that's perfect! But what if your father doesn't approve of her going behind his back? Will she be in any trouble?"

"I assure you, she will not be held responsible. This is my doing, and I will handle my father."

"Then it'll be a wonderful surprise for Gabriella. I know a dressmaker who's a whiz at alterations. She knows the situation and will work day and night if necessary. It'll be part of my gift to Gabriella."

"She will appreciate your efforts." Gratitude poured out of his softly spoken words.

"She'll be a beautiful bride."

"Yes, she will be."

The conversation ebbed, and oddly, as tired as Cara was, she didn't want it to end. "How are the plans going?"

"I have arranged for food and drink and I have musicians coming for the ceremony."

Were they the same quartet of men who'd played for her during Alex's engagement to her? The same men who'd serenaded her the night he swept her away from her office? "If it's the same four who played for us, they were very good."

"It is not."

"Too short notice for them? Oh, that's too bad. I'd imagine they'd be booked weeks in advance."

"I didn't call them, Cara. Our engagement was very special to me…to us. Those memories are only for us to share."

Her eyes slid closed. He was saying all the right things. "Oh, Alex."

"I mean it, sweetheart."

Cara didn't know what to say to that. The gesture filled her heart and she berated herself for believing him. For thinking that possibly he was telling the truth this time. The problem was, she didn't know where fake Alex ended and the real Alex began.

Her silence brought forth his deep sigh. "I can't change what happened between us. If I could, I would. But I hope your heart tells you to give us another chance."

Cara nibbled on her lower lip. "This is very hard for me."

Queasiness rocked her belly and she didn't think it was Baby del Toro causing the turmoil but rather the little one's father. The icy walls of her resistance began slowly melting.

"I know, Cara," he said solemnly. And then in an upbeat tone, he offered, "At least I brought you good news tonight. We both want to see Chance and my sister married and happy."

"Yes, that's true."

"I will see you soon. Sweet dreams to you."

Five

Five days flew by and Cara had never been so organized or exhausted in her life. The wedding plans she'd helped Gabriella with were coming together nicely. While Gabriella confirmed that Alex had taken care of the essentials for the guests, Cara made sure the bride had everything she needed. She'd helped her pick out a small bouquet of white roses surrounded by baby's breath from a wedding florist. They'd gone shoe shopping and found the most spectacular pair of ivory pumps for her to wear. Gabriella knew jewelry—the collections she'd designed turned heads—but when it came to deciding just the right pieces for her own wedding, she'd asked for Cara's opinion. Together they came up with a matching set, a mother of pearl drop necklace and bracelet that lent just the right touch of elegance.

With the details all in place, Cara had one final maid-of-honor duty to perform before the big day. And now, as

Cara made her way up the steps of Chance's home, she held a big cumbersome box in her hands. Giddy with excitement, she knocked on the door.

Gabriella opened the door with a flourish. "Cara, I'm so happy you are here. Come in. And what is this secret big surprise you have for me?"

"Chance isn't home, is he?"

Cara had conspired with Alex this morning on the telephone to make sure Chance wouldn't be at the ranch this afternoon. "Actually, no. He is still at the club with his friends."

Cara nodded. "Good. Then I can give you your surprise. Chance can't see it."

"What can you possibly surprise me with? You've already done so much," she said, while her curious gaze fixed on the big box.

"You'll see. May I?" She gestured toward the parlor.

"Certainly." Gabriella led the way, and she followed her into the room. She set the box down on the sofa and turned to Gabriella. "Please, open it. I can't wait for you to see it."

Looking skeptical, Gabriella darted glances from Cara to the box with her brows gathered. "What have you done?" she asked in a mumble as she lifted open the lid.

Gabriella's face crumpled with emotion and a surprised gasp whispered from her lips. "Oh…it's my mama's wedding gown."

She lifted the gown out of the box gently, as if it would break into tiny pieces if she wasn't careful, and turned to Cara. "It's exquisite."

"I think so, too."

"You did this?" she asked, her eyes filling with gratitude.

"I couldn't pull this off without your brother's help. He had it sent from Las Cruces."

Gabriella hugged the dress to her body and twirled around slowly. "I am amazed. I have dreamed of wearing this dress all of my life."

"And now you shall."

"But we have already purchased a wedding dress. I was to have a final fitting later today."

"That was your backup dress, in case your mother's dress didn't arrive on time. The salon consultant was in on my little plan. I hope you don't mind. I've made all the arrangements. She's on standby to do any alterations you might need and has guaranteed the gown will be ready in two days. But Gabriella, the other dress is also beautiful on you. It's really your choice."

She grinned. "Of course I will wear my mother's dress."

They both studied the dress more carefully now. In a Cinderella design with a heart-shaped neckline, cinched waist and flared skirt with an ivory lace overlay throughout, Cara could tell that Gabriella's size and shape greatly resembled Elena del Toro's. "It doesn't look like it'll need much altering."

"No?" Gabriella smiled. "Oh, Cara, I cannot thank you enough." She set the gown down carefully on the sofa and gave Cara a loving hug. "You are a good friend," she said, breaking away to look into her eyes. "I will forever remember your thoughtfulness when I think about my wedding day."

"I'm glad. Will you try it on? I'm dying to see it on you."

"*Sí*. Yes, I am anxious to wear it. Will you help me?"

"It's my duty as your maid of honor."

"Come," Gabriella said as both of them lifted the dress from different ends. "Let us see how well it fits."

Cara stepped out onto the veranda and gave Gabriella a hug. "Everything is all set. I think we've got your wedding under control. All you have to do is show up at your brother's house in two days and look beautiful. I have no doubt you will."

"You are sweet to say that, Cara."

"The dress is gorgeous. All that delicate lace. I love it. I know Chance will love it, too."

Chance and Alex strode up the path. "What will I love?" Chance took his place beside Gabriella and kissed her. "Aside from you?"

Cara hadn't noticed Alex's car pull up and she avoided looking at him now, but she sensed his intense stare. His close presence unnerved her. She'd seen Dr. Jayne Belfort yesterday and the obstetrician had asked about the baby's father's medical history. Cara told the doctor she'd take the paperwork home and have it filled out by her next appointment, but she wondered how long she could get away with hiding her pregnancy. Now her clothes were fitting snugly, and aside from buying a whole new wardrobe, Cara's days of secrecy were numbered.

"Nothing," Cara said to Chance, "that would interest you." She smiled at him. "Gabriella and I had some wedding details to go over."

"Thank you for giving us a hand in this, Cara." He set his arm around Gabriella's shoulders. "We appreciate all that you and Alex are doing for us."

Cara spared a glance at Alex and found amusement lighting his dark brown eyes. They'd both planned the ruse to get Chance out of the house. Alex wasn't supposed to deliver Chance for another thirty minutes. After a business meeting at TCC, they were to play nine holes of golf with Zach Lassiter and Josh Gordon. But they'd arrived earlier than Cara had expected and her sneaking suspicions flared. Had Alex meant to run into her here?

If he'd stuck to the timetable, Cara wouldn't be staring at his handsome face right now.

"You're welcome, Chance. It's my pleasure," she said.

"As it is mine. I'm happy if my sister is happy," Alex said.

"I am," Gabriella said, beaming with love.

"Would you two like to stay and join us for dinner?" Chance asked.

"Oh, boy," Cara said. "I would I love to, but I've got a few more things to tend to before the wedding."

"I, too, have plans for tonight," Alex said. "But thank you."

"Yeah, great golf game, Alex," Chance said with a wry smirk. "You beat us again." Chance turned to his fiancée. "Gabriella, it seems your brother's going to be funding a college scholarship for the employees' children at the club. He's made a generous proposal."

"Alejandro, I didn't know that," Gabriella said, her brows lifting. "Tell me about it."

"I didn't say anything because I wasn't sure it would be approved. But it's official now. I hope to have the details written up and the scholarship program started by next fall. I plan to name it the Elena del Toro Educational Fund."

Gabriella's lips trembled as she gazed at her brother with eyes brimming with admiration. "That's…that's… oh, Alejandro."

Alex's generosity touched Cara deeply. It wasn't just baby and hormones that stirred her emotions. Alex was honoring his mother in a beautiful way.

"It's a wonderful idea," Cara found herself saying.

"You think so, Cara?" Alex asked, his gaze soft and warm.

"Yes." Tenderness swept into her heart, an emotion she couldn't afford. "I'd better get going." She said a final farewell to everyone and dashed down the walkway leading to her car.

She was ready to open her door by the time Alex caught up. "Cara, wait."

With her hand on the handle, she turned to him. "Alex, I really have a dozen things to do—"

"Are you going to visit Mercy?"

Heat climbed her throat. The mention of her horse blistered her mind. How would she ever be able to enjoy her visits with Mercy anymore without thinking about hiding in that old office with Alex and reliving the exciting things that had happened in there? "Yes, I'm planning to make a quick stop to see Mercy. And no, I don't want any company."

The coffee-brown of his eyes darkened as a smile played on his lips. "You just let me know anytime you do need assistance in the stables," he said. "It's something I dream about at night."

His candor and the winsome tone of his voice begged her to confess that she dreamed of it, too. But she held her tongue. "I really do have to go."

"I need your help," he said as she began to turn away. "With the wedding."

"You do?" His nod and contrite expression gave him credibility. "What's wrong?"

He ran a hand along his jawline and then scratched his chin as if hating to admit something. "I didn't think hosting a small wedding would be a problem. I should've hired an event planner. I have questions about so many things. I don't want to burden my sister with the details. I want this to be perfect for her."

It was noble of him. He sounded sincere. "What details?"

Alex reached into his pocket and came up with a list.

She took the paper from his hand and glanced at a minimum of twelve questions. Cara looked up into his baffled face with a note of sympathy for him. "Looks like these things have to be addressed."

"Will you help?"

"Of course."

He breathed a sigh of relief. "Thank you."

They arranged for her to meet at his house first thing in the morning.

Cara wasn't looking forward to seeing Rodrigo del Toro, who was living there temporarily, but she did want Gabriella and Chance's wedding to be perfect.

She had that in common with Alex.

"Okay, cross number nine off the list," Cara said to Alex. "We're making headway and I can see it all coming together now."

"You do have a flair for this, Cara." Alex stood beside her in the backyard. She'd made the decision to have the ceremony on the grassy area that overlooked the Pine Valley Golf Course. The florist would decorate the gazebo, and white canvas-backed chairs would line up on either side of the aisle in rows of five. They expected no more than forty people, the closest of friends and family only.

Hors d'oeuvres and champagne would flow over into the pool area and the actual meal would be served on a large stone-and-wood patio area closest to the kitchen.

"As for decorations, the grounds are so lovely, the home so beautiful, we only need candles and flowers to set the mood. Nothing extravagant. Simple and elegant will work just fine. I'll call the florist and double-check that we're on the same page."

"Okay, number ten is history." Alex slashed another question off his list.

It was only ten in the morning. Cara might possibly make it to the office before lunch. She'd taken some time off to help plan the wedding and she didn't want her day ruined by coming up against her father's wrath.

Alex was diligent this morning, sticking to the agenda. Deep in concentration, his questions were thoughtful and intelligent. He really did need her help. He had no eye for transforming his home for a wedding event, while everything seemed to come to Cara easily. She could envision it in her mind.

Alex had made sure his father wasn't skulking around. She didn't ask, and he didn't volunteer anything except to say when he'd opened the door to her, "No need to worry. You won't be running into my father this morning." That, too, was thoughtful, and she appreciated him lessening the stress of her day.

By eleven o'clock, she and Alex had worked out all the questions on the list. She'd gone over every detail on his end and felt assured all would run smoothly. "I think the wedding will be beautiful."

Alex smiled, his focus now redirected and aimed fully at her. "I agree. You are amazing."

Alex's compliment brought tingles and comforting strokes to her battered ego. "Thank you, Alex."

He nodded. "I only speak the truth."

A new concept for him? He wasn't so keen on the truth when they'd met, but Cara didn't break the mood with that remark.

"Gabriella is thrilled about wearing our mother's wedding gown. I should've thought of it myself. You made that happen for her."

"No, I only thought of it. You made it happen."

"It wasn't so hard, was it? And now my sister is happy." She smiled and grabbed her purse from a patio table.

Slinging it over her shoulder, she began walking inside the house. "I think we're through for today. I should get to work."

"I'll walk you out." Alex put his hand to her back, escorting her through his house to the front door. He opened it and stepped onto the front steps. A path of multicolored paving stones led them to her car. She turned to say goodbye. "I guess…I'll see you at the wedding tomorrow."

He blinked, his lips sealing off a tight smile. "Yes. Tomorrow." His hand came out to rest on the right side of her face, his long brown fingertips gentle on her cheek. "I won't forget your help today."

"I didn't mind help—"

With a dip of his head, he brushed the softest, featherlike kiss onto her lips. She closed her eyes to the divine sensation and after it was over, she took a long, deep breath. Wow.

In a daze, she got into her car, and Alex closed the door for her. She pulled away, glancing at him through the rearview mirror. He stood straight and tall, his perfect espresso eyes bidding her farewell until she pulled through the mansion gates and drove onto the open road.

Later that day, Alex walked into the Cattleman's Club and came face-to-face with Paul Windsor, who'd just come in from the tennis courts. The older man spotted him and scowled. He moved quickly to head Alex off, his feet spread apart, blocking the entrance to a private meeting room.

"You're not going to get away with it, del Toro."

"Get away with what?" Alex struggled to keep his voice calm. Windsor would get what was coming to him soon.

Windsor's blue eyes were cool as steel. "You're a menace to this club. You've lied and cheated your way in and now it's time for you to leave. I helped start this club. I'm a charter member. And the last time I checked, we didn't allow frauds to run the show."

Hot, thick blood raced through Alex's veins. A pulse in his neck throbbed. He had yet to see the man who'd ordered him beaten and kidnapped until this minute. Now that he remembered everything, he wondered how such a scoundrel could father a woman like Cara. "Windsor, the last time *I* checked, I was still a member in good standing at this club."

"Don't think I won't change that."

"You've tried. It hasn't worked so far."

"You think you can buy your way back into everyone's good graces by giving away a scholarship? You won that vote by default. None of the members wanted to decline for the sake of the children. There're a lot of good people here who still want nothing to do with you, del Toro. Including my daughter. I always knew you were no good for her."

"Leave Cara out of this," Alex said, his teeth gnashing. Windsor was exaggerating. Already some members were commending his idea. He hoped other members would forgive him in time. And honestly, if his funding helped children attend college, then he wouldn't worry about what the haters had to say.

"Why should I? You used her to spy on my company. You lied to her, and I'm only grateful she had the good sense to back away from you herself when she found out your deceit. No one tries to take my company down or hurt my daughter without paying the consequences."

"Interesting how you put that, Windsor. It almost sounds like a threat. Because we all know that Chance McDaniel had nothing to do with having me kidnapped and roughed up."

"Chance is a good man. My daughter should've married him."

His hands closed into two tight fists. Windsor hit a nerve. Damn it. Chance had dated Cara and they'd been pretty serious. Then Alex had moved in the second he met her at a TCC party. Meeting her had been a slam dunk, something out of his control. He'd fallen for her fast, and she'd returned the feelings. Chance had done the honorable thing in stepping aside, but some believed his friend harbored enough bad feelings and jealousy to hurt Alex. Hopefully, some of that suspicion would be put to rest after Chance's wedding to his sister. And once Alex could get all the proof he needed for Windsor's arrest, Chance's name would finally be cleared.

Deep down, Alex often wondered if Cara wouldn't have been better off with Chance. Now, Alex knew better. Chance belonged with Gabriella the same way Alex belonged with Cara.

"You're hedging, Windsor. Everyone knows how much you hated me."

Windsor's eyes flickered. "Are you making an accusation, del Toro?"

Alex wasn't going to reveal too much yet, but he wanted to be on the spot when the arrest was finally made. The only regret he'd had in seeking justice for the crimes committed against him was that Cara would be hurt. Her father was a criminal. That news would surely alter her life. "I'm making an observation."

Wearing a polo shirt and tennis shorts, Paul Windsor hardly looked imposing. He crossed his arms over his chest, his mouth twisting into a snarl. "I thought so. You don't have anything on me."

Alex raised a brow. "Are you sure of that?"

Another flicker of doubt crossed Windsor's features. "You can't prove a thing."

"If you're innocent you have nothing to worry about, Paul. Now, step aside. I have a meeting."

"You don't scare me." But the tremor in his raspy voice gave him away.

"Maybe I should. Think about it." Alex stepped past Windsor and opened the door, leaving the man standing there befuddled.

Six

"That should do it," Cara said, fastening the last button on Gabriella's wedding gown in the guest bedroom Alex had offered for the bridal room. The gown fit Gabriella's slim body perfectly and the ivory color added lovely accents to her glowing Latin complexion. She wore only delicate flowers in hair that was swept off one shoulder and draped over the other shoulder in soft curls.

A champagne bucket and tall flutes, chocolate-dipped strawberries and pastries lay untouched on a silver platter brought in by Maria, Alex's housekeeper. Not that the lavish fare wasn't appetizing, but both of them were too excited to take a taste.

"Stunning. Wait'll Chance sees you in this dress," Cara remarked to Gabriella's reflection in the mirror. "He'll count his blessings that he was smart enough not to let you slip through his fingers."

"Thank you, Cara. I am so excited I can barely stand it.

But you are beautiful in your dress, as well. A good choice we made, wouldn't you say?"

Gabriella had picked it out, and from the second Cara tried it on, she knew it was the right one. Sewn with a handkerchief design, higher in front than back, and made of crinkle wisteria-blue chiffon, the bodice crisscrossed her chest and flared from there, hiding any thickening of her middle in an empire style. "Yes, I'm happy with the dress. But today is not about me."

She walked to the queen-size bed in Alex's guest room, picked up a white satin-ribboned bridal bouquet from the florist's box and handed it to her. "Here you go. The final touch. We are due downstairs very soon."

She gave Gabriella one last glance, her heart humming with warmth for her friend. As she held her own small bouquet of white roses, the feeling accompanied her out of the bedroom and down the staircase as she held Gabriella's hand. She met with Rodrigo del Toro's gaze at the base of the stairs.

Cara had never seen the softer side of Alex's father. But today, because Gabriella had pleaded with him to attend, and Alex had laid on the guilt, convincing him that he'd regret missing his only daughter's wedding and telling him of Gabriella's fondest wish to be married in her mother's gown with her father walking her down the aisle, Rodrigo had finally agreed. Now his eyes brimmed with pride for his daughter.

Cara gave him a rigid smile as they reached the bottom of the staircase, and he smiled graciously back.

She kissed Gabriella's cheek. "I will see you at the altar." The she turned to Rodrigo. "Mr. del Toro." She greeted him only for Gabriella's sake and then strode to the dining room to peer at the backyard filling up with guests.

Alex came to stand behind her, his presence and musky

scent filling her senses. She took a deep breath. "The yard is transformed into a beautiful garden," she said.

"Thanks to you," he said softly. His warm breath caressed the back of her neck, sending tremors throughout her body.

"Shouldn't you be with Chance?"

"I will be in a moment."

His hands slipped to her waist gently in the barest of touches and her skin prickled. She had yet to turn to him. He would be dashing. He would be perfect. Resisting him sapped her energy. "You look amazing, Cara." His nose brushed her partially upswept hair as his lips skimmed her throat. "My sister is beautiful today and I wish her well, but it is also you who should be wearing a wedding gown."

She spun around slowly. She hadn't been wrong. He was tall, dark, handsome. His eyes beckoned hope as a charming smile graced his beautiful mouth.

Weddings always made her sentimental. A flutter whispered in her stomach. She blinked. The baby? Had he moved? She froze, hoping to feel it again. Hoping the sweet sensation would ripple through her once more.

"Cara?"

How just like Alex to charm movement from his child on such a sentimental day. If anyone could do it, it would be him. But surely it was too soon to feel any flutters yet. She must have imagined it. Whatever it was, the baby's presence softened her outlook on everything. Cara nurtured new life. Her baby thrived. Her hands, locked at her sides, hid her secret when she wanted to touch her belly and offer her love.

She batted her eyes. "What? Is it time?"

"Yes, the music is playing. I will see you later."

He kissed her cheek and disappeared through the kitchen doors.

Cara grinned and caressed her stomach now.

It was a monumental day for her.

In so many ways.

Vows were spoken under a floral archway of roses and greenery. Cara witnessed two of her dear friends speak promises of love and devotion. The sweet words of dedication filled her eyes with moisture and she sniffled a few times during the ceremony.

After the deacon pronounced Chance and Gabriella husband and wife and the ceremony concluded, Alex was first to make a move. He approached her as best man to lead the small procession away from the altar. She slipped her arm though his and they walked down the white carpeted aisle. A photographer's camera clicked away at the precious moments.

Once the photographer moved on to capture the newly married couple and they were out of view of the guests, Alex lifted her into his arms. Her feet came off the ground six inches as he twirled her around. His grin was contagious, and she threw her head back and laughed along with him.

He set her down carefully. "I've missed laughing with you."

"You're crazy, Alex."

"You like that about me."

She swallowed and stared at him.

"I'm happy. My sister is married. And I'm here with you."

"Oh, Alex." She didn't know what to say to him. She was in a beautifully sentimental mood and didn't want to spoil it with condemnation.

His white teeth flashed in another infectious smile. "Tell me you're happy, Cara."

She nodded. "Yes."

"Then let's not allow anything to spoil that. Let's enjoy the day."

Around her, the din of quietly enthusiastic guests conversing, floral scents and soft music playing in the background helped her make the decision. "Yes, I would like that."

Gabriella strolled up, her face beaming and her fingers entwined with her new groom's.

"Congratulations, you two!" Cara hugged the bride first and whispered in her ear. "I'm so happy for you."

After Alex shook Chance's hand, Cara wrapped her arms around the groom's neck and spoke quietly in his ear. "You made the right choice. You and Gabriella are perfect for each other. I know you'll have a wonderful life."

Chance kissed her cheek. "I'm planning on that. Gonna start by taking her on a secret honeymoon come this summer. Someplace where we'll have a whole lot of privacy for weeks."

"Where will we go?" Gabriella asked, her eyes sparkling.

"I'm not sharing that information with anyone but you," Chance replied, wiggling his brows at her. "It'll be my wedding gift to you."

"I think I will like your surprise."

"I'm thinking you will, too."

Rodrigo stepped up and the conversation stalled. He took his daughter's hand. "You are a vision of beauty in your mother's gown, Gabriella. Seeing you wearing it has brought back many good memories."

"Oh, Papa," she said.

He squeezed her tight, both arms encircling her shoulders, and then kissed her cheek, his rigid face softening with fatherly love. Cara saw tears form, but he wiped them away immediately. "You are my baby. And now you are a wife."

He turned to Chance and extended his hand. "A handshake to welcome you to our family. I expect you will take good care of my daughter."

Chance shook his hand. "She will not have an unhappy day, if I can help it."

Rodrigo appeared appeased and nodded. Joaquin, Gabriella's onetime bodyguard who now worked for Chance, moved beside him. He wore a dogged expression that spoke of loyalty and dedication. He was here as a guest, but Cara noted his gaze on every person in attendance in silent assessment. He was still watching out for Gabriella as if the action was ingrained in him through his affection for her.

Other guests approached to congratulate the couple and Cara took the opportunity to sneak away from the group. She headed to the bathroom and locked herself in. With her palms flat on the cool marble counter, she stared at herself in the mirror as emotions swept through her. Slight quivers brought her breath up short and wrung out some of her strength. What was wrong with her?

She wasn't feeling weak. She couldn't blame out-of-whack hormones altering her perspective. She didn't believe her pregnancy alone caused this reaction. It was seeing Gabriella glowing with happiness and Chance so smitten he could hardly stand it that nudged her into thinking about her own future. It was seeing Rodrigo here, the man who'd plotted to take over Windsor Oil. It was being so close to Alex again and having his words tunneling through her mind, *"It is also you who should be wearing a wedding gown."*

All of it had gotten to her.

At times, she didn't know where to turn. Her brain told

her not to allow Alex back into her life, while her heart told her otherwise.

She turned on the faucet and filled a cup from a stack Alex kept in the cabinet. Sipping water slowly, she lowered herself down on the toilet seat and closed her eyes. She just needed a minute to gather her wits. She would take her time. She had the entire reception to get through.

And she wanted to be happy today.

It was ten minutes later when she walked out of the bathroom feeling better. Her little mental pep talk had worked. Her mind was made up. She wouldn't allow anything negative to get to her today. She'd deal with her emotions tomorrow…and the next day and the day after that. But for today, she would enjoy her maid-of-honor duties and pretend she hadn't a care in the world.

"Are you okay?" Alex said, approaching her with a worried expression.

She smiled. "I'm fine."

His gaze roamed her face as if searching for the truth. She kept her smile in place and didn't refuse the hand he extended. She took it and strolled outside with him as dusk settled on the horizon and table candles sent shards of flickering light skyward.

Toasts were given, the meal was served and as the band resumed playing, Chance and Gabriella were called up to the parquet dance floor for their first dance.

"They will call us up next. Will you dance with me?" Alex asked.

"Of course," she said. "It's part of my duty as maid of honor to dance with the best man."

Alex arched a brow. "And it's part of my duty to make sure you enjoy yourself tonight."

"It's not your duty, Alex. But I am enjoying myself."

Alex laid a hand on her waist, drawing her close. His

touch seeped into her skin, and she relaxed against him, placing her head on his shoulder. His lips tickled her ear and tingles broke out on her throat where his warm breath caressed her. "I want to see you happy, Cara."

Her jittery nerves had finally calmed from her little panic attack in the bathroom.

The invitation to join the bride and groom in a dance was announced and Alex led her to the floor, her hand locked in his grip. She was swept into his arms smoothly, and Alex's fluid grace wasn't difficult to follow as he moved and swayed with the music. His dark dreamy eyes focused solely on her. She was barely aware of Gabriella and Chance nearby or anyone else, for that matter. She wasn't up to fighting Alex's charm tonight. He was her escort, her other half in the bridal party, and she couldn't possibly avoid him. They'd been thrown together all night.

Halfway during the song, the rest of the guests were invited to the dance floor and soon they were surrounded. She danced with Alex for half an hour nonstop after that and was only given a breather when Alex tapped Chance on the shoulder so he could dance with his sister.

Chance glanced at her. "Shall we?"

She sighed. "If you don't mind, I'd love to sit this one out."

"I don't mind." He led her to the table. "Would you like a drink…of cranberry juice?" He smiled. "I noticed that's all you've been drinking tonight."

"No, thank you. I'm juiced out." She'd already had two glasses of juice, and after dancing with Alex five songs' worth, an ice-cold glass of water looked really tempting. "I'll have water." She lowered herself into a seat, and he sat next to her. "Does it look odd that I was only drinking juice?"

"Not to me. You aren't a big drinker and juice is real

good for you." He paused and leaned in, lowering his voice. "How's the baby doing?"

"I saw the doctor and she said all was going well. I'm healthy and the baby is growing. Tonight, I think…" She nibbled on her lip. Why did her good news bring so much guilt? Possibly because under normal circumstances she would be reporting this news to the baby's father.

"What do you think, Cara?"

"Well, I, uh…I think I felt the baby move."

"Really?"

"I know it's early yet and I might be imagining it, but it really felt like movement."

"Well, darn if that isn't exciting. I can't wait until Gabriella and I start a family."

"It's an amazing feeling, Chance."

His head dipped to meet her at eye level. "But now I see you're frowning."

"It's not an ideal situation," she admitted, drawing in her lower lip. "I haven't forgiven Alex. I'm not even sure I really know Alejandro del Toro."

Chance unfastened his tie and unbuttoned the top two buttons on his shirt. "I get that…if he wasn't Gabriella's brother I don't know if he wouldn't be nursing a broken arm or leg, maybe even a rib or two."

Cara laughed. Chance was full of bluster.

"He did throw us a humdinger of a wedding though."

"He did."

"And you helped quite a bit."

She nodded and glanced at Gabriella on her brother's arm. They were heading over to the table, a picture of stately grace, elegance and Latin good looks. "Here comes your bride."

"My wife," Chance agreed. His face lit up.

Cara sipped her drink, grateful that before reaching the

table, Alex was called away from someone on the wait-staff. She spent the next thirty minutes with the bride and groom. Chance went on and on about their plans for the future, holding Gabriella's hand as she gave nods of approval. The two were truly in sync with each other. Their marriage would be a good one.

By the end of the evening, after most of the guests had gone home and Cara had said her farewells to the bride and groom, she was totally beat and ready to fall into bed.

Alex walked her outside. He kept his hand possessively on her waist as they strolled toward the valet retrieving the guests' cars. His attentiveness tonight reminded her of the couple they'd once been. It hurt to think how her life might've turned out differently if he hadn't lied to her.

"I'll drive you home," he announced.

With her defenses down and a sentimental mood humming through her body, being alone with Alex wouldn't be a wise move. "Thank you, but it's not necessary. I have my car."

His drew a deep breath. "Cara...I want to spend more time with you." The words were soft and smooth, but there was no mistaking his frustration.

"I just can't, Alex." Somehow, over the past few days, her anger at him had faded and all that was left was desolation over what might have been.

"I won't press you, but know that my door is always open to you. Anytime, day or night."

His sweet words only added to her heartache. If only he'd given her good reason to trust him again, but she didn't think that was possible anymore. "I'll remember that."

"We had a good time tonight. Remember that, as well." He pressed a featherlike kiss on the mouth, and her lips trembled from the soft touch. "I surely will not forget it."

* * *

"Thanks for not picking up Paul Windsor at his house, Nate. I don't want Cara to witness him being arrested," Alex said, standing on the steps of the Texas Cattleman's Club. "It's going to be enough of a shock to her when she hears the news." Just three days ago he was dancing with Cara at his sister's wedding. And now, in just a short time, she'd find out about her father's crimes. For weeks after his accident, she'd been horrified that someone would commit such a vile act against him. Learning it was her father's doing would surely tilt her world off its axis.

"Yeah, it's gonna be rough on her. Are you planning on telling her yourself?"

Alex nodded. "I hope to. I am worried about her reaction. He's not the greatest father, but he is all she has," Alex said on a sigh. "I wish to God it didn't have to be this way. I have no doubt he'll deny everything."

"He'll lawyer up immediately, no matter where we make the arrest," Nate added. "We'll give him a chance to confess. If we lay out all the cards on the table, he might want to do the smart thing. We pretty much have him nailed. The man he hired cut a deal for a lesser sentence. He's naming names. There were three men involved with your abduction. He's giving us what we need to put Windsor away for a long time. But he's claiming Windsor only wanted you out of the picture. He wanted you roughed up. We can prove kidnapping, but probably not attempted murder."

"At least that's some consolation for Cara." Alex sighed. "But he's still a dangerous man who thinks he's above the law."

"Well, the law's about to come down on him," Nate said. "It'd be better if you weren't here, Alex."

He nodded. "I understand. But I wish I could see the look on his face when you haul him in." He gestured toward the dining room. "He's in there having dinner with a few of his cronies."

"Okay," Nate said. "Sit tight. I'll call you later. Until then, don't say a word to anyone."

"All right. Good luck."

Alex watched the sheriff enter the premises. Sighing under his breath, he was relieved that Paul Windsor would no longer be a threat to him. The cagey old man would not be causing him any more trouble.

He walked away and climbed into his Ferrari. Leaning his head against the seat, he took a moment to stare out the window. His mind flashed images of his attack and kidnapping. His heart pumped hard as he recalled being beaten then blindfolded and driven somewhere. When he came to, he hadn't known where he was or if he was going to be killed. He'd been left alone in that house to wonder and that had been the worst feeling of all.

A chilling shudder rippled through his body.

It was all Windsor's doing.

If he hadn't intervened, Alex would have told Cara the truth about himself and cleared everything up. They would have been married by now. Alex shook his head. Too bad it had to come to this. Cara's father would be lost to her now.

With a press of a button, the engine roared to life. He pulled out of his parking spot, his car handling the turns easily as his heart grew heavy with thoughts of Cara. He winced, grinding his teeth as he pictured Cara's crestfallen face when she heard the news.

He took the long route home and every so often glanced at his phone. Nate told him to sit tight. He couldn't do that, so he kept on driving. An hour later, he pulled up in front of his house and parked the car. He waited impatiently, strumming his fingers along the dashboard and nearly jumped out of his skin when his cell phone rang. *"Dios!"*

He answered the phone.

"It's done," Nate said.

"He's in jail?" Alex asked.

"Yes. He's being processed as we speak."

"How did it go at the club?"

"He was dumbfounded and made all kinds of excuses to his dinner partners, saying it was a big misunderstanding. After he was read his rights, he had the gall to tell one his friends he'd see him tomorrow on the golf course."

"Once he finds out we've rounded up witnesses who are willing to testify against him, his mind won't be on sinking a putt," Alex said.

"True. Your father and his men worked fast getting us the lead we needed to make the arrest. You can thank him for that. Windsor's bail will be high, but I've no doubt he'll raise the money. I don't think he'll go after you…he's got enough problems, but watch your back, Alex. Just in case."

"I plan to. I will not be caught off my guard again. Thank you for the call."

Alex pushed End and stared at the blank screen. It was done. Paul Windsor's crimes were exposed. He would be put away for a long time.

Alex strode into the house, his nerves on edge as he made his way into the great room. He found his father seated in the leather recliner, his cell phone to his ear, rattling off a list of commands in Spanish.

Rodrigo looked up and finished his call abruptly. He stood and walked over to him, placing a hand on his shoulder. "Alejandro, I have news."

"What's that?"

"I am needed at home. I will be leaving tonight. I have only stayed this long to make sure my children are safe. But I have neglected my duties at home long enough. I wish you to come home. Join me in Mexico."

"No, Papa. We have been through this before, and you know I cannot return to Mexico. My place is here now."

"The woman?"

"Cara, yes. I have to work things out with her."

Rodrigo frowned. He didn't try to hide his disappointment. "My children have abandoned me."

"We are happy here."

"Your sister, yes. She is married now. But you, Alejandro, what do you have here?"

"I have friends and a business of my own. I have the woman I want to marry. I cannot leave her now. I have news, too. Her father has been arrested. Just tonight. He was taken to jail."

Rodrigo's face brightened and he squeezed Alex's shoulder. "May he rot in there for what he's done to you."

"He may very well."

A satisfied gleam entered his father's eyes. "*Sí.* But is it enough for what you have lost?"

"It has to be, Papa. I am greatly relieved and satisfied. I will work out the rest in time. You can go home to Las Cruces knowing justice will be served."

His father's mouth twisted and frown lines appeared. Rodrigo did not let go of things easily. Unsettled by his expression, Alex gave him a direct look. "It is done. We must move on with our lives."

"Humph."

Alex was sorry about the whole damn mess. If he hadn't agreed to his father's scheme to begin with then none of this would have happened. "Papa, give up your idea to buy out Windsor Energy."

His father's eyes flickered with a dark glint. "We shall see, Alejandro. We shall see."

"You have caused enough trouble. Go home and enjoy your life. Forget about the takeover."

His father set his jaw. "I cannot make you that promise right now. But I must go. I have other business that has been neglected."

Alex shook his head. Damn the old man. He was stubborn. If Alex challenged him tonight, pride would make Rodrigo take further action. It was best to let him go now without pressuring him. He'd deal with him later. With his father gone, he stood a better chance of winning Cara back.

He sighed. "I will drive you to the airport."

"It is not necessary. I have a driver ready to take me to see Gabriella. From there, I will leave. And you," his father said in a softer voice as he placed his palm to Alex's face, "you must do what compels you, my son."

"*Sí*. It is what I intend to do."

Cara had to do some serious pulling of strings to get in to see her father after his arrest. Paul Windsor had powerful friends and one of them had come through for her. Now, she sat in an old overstuffed leather chair and faced her father across a metal table. A jailhouse guard was posted outside the small sterile room and she was granted ten minutes to visit him. As she peered into his weary blue eyes, the truth of his guilt apparent in his sheepish expression, her body slipped farther down into the lumpy seat cushion. "Is it true, Dad? Did you have Alex run off the road and almost killed?"

He glanced around the empty room as if the walls had ears and lowered his voice. "It wasn't like that, Cara."

She trembled as hope for his denial was dashed. "You hired thugs to do your dirty work. One of them confessed."

"I'm not a murderer, Cara."

"But you did have Alex run off the road in his car. You had your men b-beat him," Cara choked out. The words were hard to say. To associate her father with the awful crimes was unbearable. "They took him across the border, tied him up and left him there. He didn't know if he was going to be executed. He didn't know where he was."

"Cara, calm down." Again, he glanced around the room. "I only wanted him away from you for a while so you would come to your senses."

"I loved him."

"He was a fraud. He was out to snatch my company away."

Cara rose from her seat, stunned. Now it made perfect sense. "You knew?" She wished to God it wasn't true. But her father's motives became shockingly clear. "You knew who Alex was before anyone else did and decided to have him beaten and dragged away instead of trusting me to do the right thing?"

"Not so loud, Cara." He hung his head and rubbed his hand down his face. "I'm in big trouble. I need you by my side on this."

"H-how can you ask that of me?" Cara's legs wouldn't hold her another second. She lowered into the seat again. "You could've told me what you knew about Alex. I would've confronted him. I would've gotten to the truth."

Her father shook his head. "You were besotted."

"You give me no credit."

"He was using you, and you were too blind to see it."

Her father's perception of her was almost a bigger injury than his betrayal. "How did you find out about him?"

He shrugged. "I have my sources."

Leaning forward, she met his direct gaze. "How, Dad?"

He sighed. "I suspected something was up when you started dating a man who'd shown up in Royal out of the blue, making investment deals with club members who've been around a long time, nudging his way into relationships. I keep my enemies close. I knew Rodrigo del Toro was sniffing around Windsor Energy and I'd heard about his son, a handsome young man who worked for him. He'd fallen off the map in Mexico two years ago and he was the same age and had the same appearance as Alex Santiago. I trusted my instincts, Cara. It's something you need to learn."

Tears swelled in Cara's eyes. "This is horribly unbelievable. I don't…" She caught a sob in her throat. "I don't know what to say…"

He reached for her hand, but she was warned from any physical contact in the room. Which was a good thing—she didn't want to comfort her dad. She didn't know him. She sat staring at the man who'd raised her and couldn't comprehend his ruthlessness.

Alex had suffered at his hands. But so had she. She'd been betrayed by both men she'd loved, and took part of the blame for being such a fool to believe in the two of them. "You're right about one thing, Dad. You are in big trouble. Kidnapping across the border is a serious federal offense."

"I've hired the best attorney money can buy. He comes highly recommended."

"I think you're going to need it."

A fleeting thought came to mind. She'd been too busy thinking about the crimes her father had committed to think about his company. The scandal could be devastating. The shame and bad press brought to Windsor Energy could bring the company crashing down. The whole thing would be fodder for the media. The company her father tried so hard to protect might fall to ruin. It was on her shoulders now to pick up the pieces. Cara couldn't deal with that at the moment. It was too much. "I have to go."

"Cara…button, I need you."

Her heart ached so badly. It wouldn't be long before her father's friends turned their backs on him. If convicted, he'd be a known felon. Bad press would follow anyone associated with him. Now he was reaching out to her. Too little, too late. She wouldn't abandon her father but she wouldn't defend him, either. He'd done a terrible thing. "It's going to take me some time to deal with all of this. Take care of yourself. I'll be back soon to visit. I love you, Dad."

Cara exited the room, choking back sobs. Her stomach churned bitter acid and she dashed out of the premises without saying a word to anyone. Her cell phone had started ringing just an hour after her father's arrest. She'd shut it off. She couldn't speak with anyone tonight. She headed straight home, ignoring her voice-mail messages, and prayed like hell the gates to Windsor Farms wouldn't be swarming with reporters.

Her prayers were answered as she pulled undisturbed into the stately gates of her home and they automatically closed behind her. A pent-up breath released from her throat—she was in the clear. Official news of her father's arrest hadn't yet been made public, though it had spread like wildfire through the Cattleman's Club. The news would hit front and center tomorrow morning. She had tonight to shut herself off from the world and protect herself from scrutiny and the questions she didn't know how to answer.

As soon as she entered the cottage, her shoulders slumped and she sighed with relief. Familiar surroundings comforted her. At least she could hide out behind the Windsor walls for a time. But she was a realist and understood the gravity of the situation was a heavy weight for her to carry all alone.

She tossed her purse and tan blazer onto the parlor sofa and then lowered onto it. As she leaned forward, her hands came to rest on her cheeks and she swallowed a heavy gulp of air. "Oh, Dad," she whispered, "why did you do it?"

She gave her head a shake. She'd never understand what possessed him to take such drastic measures. Now that he'd been arrested, he'd most likely go to prison for a long time and would never know his grandchild. Cara squeezed her eyes closed. Her baby would never have the love of his or her grandfather. They would never bond or spend time together.

How would she ever explain her father's absence to her child? What could she say? Your grandfather hated your father so much he had him beaten then dumped over the border and is now serving out a prison term for his crimes?

A black cloud of uncertainty loomed overhead. The baby came first and then she'd have to deal with the fallout at Windsor Energy.

"But not tonight," she said quietly.

Cara wanted a shred of peace.

She wanted to forget and she knew there was only one thing that would help her do that.

She fished into her purse and lifted out her cell.

Alex had left her two voice mails and three texts. She dialed his number and he answered on the first ring.

"You changed the code to your gate." His smooth baritone voice didn't hide his irritation. After the first time he'd shown up here, making his way through the gates without any problem, she'd had the code changed to prevent it from happening again. Now only the people she trusted, a handful of them, could visit her unannounced.

"I... Yes, I did."

He sighed wearily and she pictured him running a hand down his face. "I couldn't get in to see you."

"You tried?"

"I tried, yes. I've been calling you and leaving messages. I know about your father, Cara. I'm sorry it turned—"

"I don't want to talk about my father," she said, biting her lower lip.

He met her comment with silence. She heard his breathing, rapid pulls of breath carrying over the phone line.

"I need to see you, Alex."

He lowered his voice. "I am close by."

"Come over."

"I will be right there."

Seven

The distant howling of a coyote didn't distract Cara as she opened the door to Alex's gorgeous dark-lashed brown eyes. The affection and concern she found in them penetrated through her. His appearance on her doorstep just minutes after her phone call touched something profound and wondrous in her heart. He hadn't lied to her. He *was* close by and he'd come to her.

He wore dark tailored dress pants, trendy Italian shoes and a shirt made of white silk pushed up to the elbows. Thick, shiny, black hair spoke of his Latino roots and his brown skin was smooth and bronzed by the Texas sun.

"Cara."

She trembled at the low, amazingly sympathetic timbre of his voice. "A-Alex, I'm glad you came."

"I will always come for you, sweetheart."

If only she could trust in that. If only her heart wasn't

still profoundly broken. If only her father's crimes hadn't multiplied her pain. "Come in," she said, stepping aside.

As he brushed past her, the scent of his expensive cologne wafted by, bringing safely harbored memories of happier times to her mind. Coming face-to-face with Alex had its drawbacks. He was eye-catching and beautiful.

"I know you didn't want to speak about your father on the phone," he said softly, "but this has got to really hurt you. When I found out the truth, my first thoughts were of you."

Cara hardened her heart to his apologies for betraying her, but tonight she did appreciate the effort he made to consider her feelings. "Alex, I don't want to speak of my father tonight. Except to say I'll be eternally sorry for his alleged crimes against you. He hasn't confessed, but he's been caught." She moved toward him and touched his cheek. His skin was warm and inviting. He turned his head and kissed her hand tenderly, his lips silky smooth. "You suffered because of me. My father must've thought he was protecting me and his company, but what he did to you was…was the worst kind of terrible."

"I cannot disagree."

"I don't know what else to say…it's all too much for me."

"He is not the man you thought he was," he said soberly.

Or maybe he was. Cara had always known her father had flaws to his character, she'd just never realized the scope of his obsession with his company or his calculated brutality. What daughter could possibly think it of the man who'd raised her? "Let's leave it at that."

"Cara," Alex said, inching closer. His presence encircled her, and she knew she hadn't made a bad decision in asking him to come over. As he cupped her elbows in his hands and drew her nearer, her skin sizzled with unbridled heat. "I am sorry for everything that has happened."

"Please…don't, Alex. I am not ready to forgive you."

He began nodding. "All right. I will not press you. But if you didn't ask me over here to speak about your father's deeds and you will not accept my apologies, why did you ask me here?"

"Remember when you said you were available to me day or night?"

His brows furrowed. Puzzlement crossed his features. "Yes. I do. And I am."

Clearly, he didn't get it. She was going to have to spell it out for him. She'd pictured this going more smoothly when she'd played it out in her mind. She needed his strength, his comfort to help her forget about this whole mess, if only for a short while.

"Well, th-that's what I want. What I need is for you to hold me and m-make love to me. I need tonight to be on my terms. With no expectation of the future, no redemption of the past." She sighed. She wouldn't lose her nerve now. "I'm asking for a, a *booty call*."

Alex's eyes opened wider and his mouth twitched, but he didn't dare smile. He wanted to. She saw his lips tighten against a grin. Had she amused him? Suddenly, it seemed like a very bad idea. She spun around and took a step away.

Instantly, his arm snaked around her waist. He pulled her up tight against him so her back brushed his chest. His voice was velvet, his lips soft on her throat. His other arm came around her waist and now she was enclosed by his powerful male heat. "You run because you think I do not want you?"

"I don't know, Alex. I can't promise you anything in return."

He stroked the sides of her torso with both hands, gliding them up and down the material of her simple A-line black dress. Her eyes closed to the pleasure.

"I do not want anything in return," he whispered, warm breath fanning over her. "I am glad you called me when you sought comfort."

She turned in his arms. Unable to meet his eyes, she stared at the golden-brown skin peeking through his open collar. "As long as you know this is only about…sex. And only for tonight."

He tipped her chin and brought his mouth down to hers in a brief kiss. Still, her lips tingled when it was over. "If you called any other man, I would have to hunt him down."

Her breath rushed out in a whoosh. "I wouldn't do that."

"I know. You need only me and I am here…for sex." He smiled.

He was impossibly charming.

"I need to forget. I need to go to a place that will stop my mind from spinning. I need to—"

"You need…me."

Her throat tightened.

"I will be what you need tonight, sweetheart."

He turned from her and walked away. Was he leaving? She tried not to panic as he moved toward the door. The overhead light flicked off and he returned to her in a room lit only by moonlight. He reached for her hand, entwined their fingers and led her to the parlor. "Come, we will start in here."

Her icy fear instantly melted. His words layered over her, giving her relief. He wouldn't leave her tonight, despite what her father had done to him. Alex lowered onto the sofa and then guided her onto his lap. She faced him at an angle, staring at his strongly sculpted profile. He adjusted her legs to rest on his and her upper body was supported by his strong arms.

"Cara, you are so beautiful," he said on a rasp.

Her fingers grazed the smooth skin of his face, giving him her silent thanks. She was grateful for his tenderness. "Already I feel so much calmer."

A wicked glint entered his eyes. "We shall see how calm you are in a few minutes."

He lowered her in his arms and brushed her lips gently with his mouth. He tasted as delicious as her favorite molten-chocolate dessert. It was a long, sweet, amazing kiss. Tension oozed out of her pores, and her limbs relaxed. He soothed her arms with his gentle touch, his fingertips applying light pressure up and down as he continued to hold her, kiss her. "You were meant to be mine," he whispered in her ear.

Goose bumps erupted as she shivered with pleasure. She *would* be his for tonight.

He took care with her, treating her like something precious, something that needed nurturing. He wouldn't disappoint her. He claimed her lips again and again, each kiss giving more promise, more heady pleasure. "Open for me," he ordered.

Cara separated her lips, and he touched his tongue to hers. A moan rose up her throat as he swept through the hollows of her mouth. She squirmed in her seat, her battered body coming alive with pings of awareness. Her mind went into shutdown mode of anything that wasn't Alex.

He was the comfort food she craved.

His kisses became more demanding in an exquisite sort of way. Tender yet tough. Gentle yet potent. He had expert hands. They roamed over her body, creating erogenous zones everywhere he touched, pinpoints of extreme sensation. She rocked in his arms, unable to hold still, unable to keep her body from falling into his rhythm.

His mouth moved down, moistening her chin with his

tongue, kissing the underside of her throat. She arched in his arms, giving him the access he required to continue his quest. His lips found the base of her throat as one hand came under her breast. He gave a gentle squeeze, and her groin pulsed. "You feel so good, Cara. I've missed you."

"Alex," she uttered, unable to formulate anything else.

She reached for the button on his silk shirt, and he clasped her wrist. "No, baby. Not yet."

She felt herself being lowered onto the sofa. "Just lie here, close your eyes and enjoy."

Her eyes feathered closed.

He lifted one shoe off her foot, and then the other. While one hand remained on her waist, the other rubbed the arch of her foot. He worked his hand on both feet, gliding over them many times. Her breathing steadied to perfectly even puffs as he stroked her arches and ankles. Endorphins eased gently through her body as he continued up her legs, gliding his hands over her sensitized skin. "You are as soft as I remember. Does this feel good?"

She nodded, and a little noise of agreement slipped through her lips.

The hem of her dress was lifted to her waist, exposing her thighs and black panties. She heard Alex draw air into his lungs as his hands traveled over her knees. His palms caressed her softest skin, inching his way higher and higher. Moisture beaded her forehead. The anticipation was killing her. He pushed his hand between her legs to separate them and his fingers brushed over her panties. "Do you want this?" he asked.

"Y-yes, oh, yes." She couldn't think of anything she wanted more.

His finger dipped into the waistband of her panties, and he lowered them down in one gliding motion. One edge of material hooked at her feet, and Cara gave a little kick to shed them entirely.

Alex chuckled from deep in his throat and the beautiful sound echoed against the walls. He adjusted his position on the sofa and lifted her hips as he moved her legs farther apart. Her pulse pounded hard in her chest, the beat ringing in her ears. He brought his head to her core and claimed her with possessive thrusts of his tongue.

Jolts of electricity shocked through her as he suckled. She tried to bolt up, but his grip on her hips tightened and she lowered down, seized by mind-blowing sensations.

Her orgasm came quick and hard.

She'd asked for a booty call.

And Alex had delivered.

Was still delivering.

Alex scooped Cara up from the sofa, and she draped her arms around his neck as he carried her toward the bedroom. She fit him perfectly in so many ways, but none more so than now. They belonged together and he would spend all night proving that to her. She was hurting, disillusioned by a father she didn't really know—a man who'd brought scandal and disappointment to her life. Alex blamed himself for her sweeping sadness, as well. Nothing mattered to him more than easing Cara's pain and showing her that she could depend on him and that he was a man she could trust again. He wouldn't let her go through this alone. When she'd called on him to come over, hope had eagerly quivered in his veins.

Cradling her to his chest, her satisfied sigh was like a kitten's purr. He kissed the top of her head and entered her room. It smelled like her. A sweetly erotic scent perfumed the air. He pushed aside half a dozen decorative pillows and lowered her down crossways on a smooth lavender bedcover. Her blond strands fanned out, framing her face in an array of honey wheat. Her black dress inched up her thighs. *Dios,* she was a picture of every dream he'd ever had.

I will never hurt you again, he thought. But Cara did not need his declarations right now. Tonight was all about making her forget. He came down on one knee beside her to stare into eyes still glowing from her first orgasm. He smiled. There would be more.

"Undress me, Cara. I want your hands on my skin."

Slowly, Cara rose up to begin to unbutton his shirt.

He bunched her hair into his fist and pushed the long golden locks behind one shoulder. He saw her face better now, her swollen lips and the rosy hue of her cheeks.

She finished the buttons and he helped her remove his shirt. Her eyes widened with admiration as she peered over the breadth of his chest. Then her mouth dropped open when her gaze traveled to her name scrolled in ink on his upper right arm. "Oh…I didn't expect…" she whispered, lifting puzzled eyes his way. She gave her head a little shake. "When did you do that?"

"When my memory returned."

She stared deeper into his eyes. "Alex."

"That's how much you mean to me. I didn't have a doubt in my head when I had your name inked on my skin. You are the only woman for me. I am the only man for you."

"I, um—" she nibbled on her lip and glanced away "—I can't hear this now."

"I know." Alex understood what tonight was about. He had no illusions of her forgiving and forgetting because he'd satisfied one need in her. But getting naked with her meant her seeing the etching on his skin that was life-lasting.

He undid his belt buckle, and her attention returned to him. There was no mistaking the hunger in her eyes. She removed his belt, tossing it to the floor, and quickly laid her hands on him. Her palms were cool against his heated flesh, and she murmured, "You feel so good, Alex."

She brushed a kiss to the skin above his waist. His lust for her doubled. He'd waited so long for her to come back to him. He didn't want to rush anything, but telling that to the parts of his body that were swelling with need wasn't working.

His hands went into her hair again, ruffling the spun silk, gripping and grasping the locks as she continued her assault on his torso. Below that area, he grew hard as stone.

She licked along the center of his torso, planting wet, hot kisses, and he sucked in oxygen. No woman had ever made him feel this way. It was even more beautiful that she took enjoyment in his body.

She rose on her knees to face him, then lifted an arm behind her and skillfully unzipped her dress. With his help, it cascaded over her shoulders, and he worked her clothes down until she was bared to him.

"Cara." He ran his hands along her arms, absorbing the texture and her softness. Her fair, creamy skin contrasted against the brown tones of his own body. "It is unfair how beautiful you are."

"It's the same for me," she said, her eyes fluttering over him. "I can't believe how much I want you right now."

"It is all I want, as well…for tonight."

She moved closer and brought her lips to hover near his mouth. "Make me forget everything, Alex."

He slipped his hands to her waist and inched them up, closer and closer to her chest. "Like this?"

She squeezed her eyes shut. The words moved through her lips slowly. "Exactly like that."

Alex strummed his thumbs over her nipples, and she sighed softly as they formed pretty twin peaks. She was fuller than usual and more sensitive than he remembered. He was careful fondling her, his palms itching to cup and mold and squeeze, but he was also unwilling to hurry anything, unwilling to be selfish. Cara was at his mercy, and he wanted to make it good for her. He wanted to make sure she'd never forget this late-night booty call.

Her parted lips tempted him, and he tasted from them again and again as he moved his hands over her body, covering every inch of her he could reach in this position. She was breathing hard, and her uttered little sighs were getting to him.

Alex lowered her down on the bed and shed his pants hastily, coming to lie beside her. There was much more he wanted to explore, much more he wanted to do to please her.

"No more, Alex." In a voice filled with want, she implored him, her hands reaching out for him. "I need you now."

"You have me."

He meant it in every sense. Cara wouldn't want for anything again. He was here, ready to make her his. It was something he'd wanted since the day he'd met her.

It was only a few seconds before Alex was shed of the rest of his clothes and sheathed with protection. He rose above her, relishing her hot, hungry hands on his chest, the pliancy of her willing body.

He would make this good for her.

He would bring them both home.

Tucked in Alex's arms, cradled by his hard body, Cara's waking was something she wanted desperately to prolong. She closed her eyes to dawning light beginning to peek into the room and nestled closer to him. In his sleep, he drew her nearer, and she silently cooed. She wasn't ready to face the day yet. Last night, she'd put her cell phone on Mute and taken her home phone off the hook.

Alex's quiet breaths hummed through the room and the sound was like a musical symphony to her ears. He'd been remarkable during the night. She couldn't have asked for more. He'd taken her to what she affectionately called the Alex Zone. He made her forget her troubles, giving her Zen moments and *other moments* she wouldn't soon forget.

If only she could live in this beautifully erotic world he'd created for her, with no past to deal with, no future to worry about. Last night, Alex had kept them in the here and now, giving her exactly what she'd needed. Cara wasn't ready…she just wasn't ready to wake from the sex coma Alex had put her in.

His arm snaked around her waist, and one eye lazily opened to her. "Mmm. Good morning, beautiful." Another tug brought her breasts to his chest.

"Oh!" He'd surprised her. "I didn't think you were awake."

"You mean because you nearly killed me last night?" He brushed a kiss to her forehead, then to her mouth.

"I thought you'd need more rest."

A rumble of sexy amusement rose from his chest. "Sleeping is overrated."

"I think so, too. I, uh— Do you need to be anywhere this morning?"

"Yes. I need to be right here with you."

Cara flopped back against the bed. A satin-covered pillow cushioned her head. "I was hoping you would say that."

"Why?"

She stared at the silver-plated art deco tiled ceiling. "I'm not ready to face the day yet."

The bed rustled and the next thing she knew, Alex was hovering over her, his day-old beard sinister looking and so extremely appealing. His hands braced on the bed beside her head and his naked self nudged her in all the right places. "Then don't."

"Really? You'll stay?"

"Until you kick me out."

"Last night was incredible," she whispered.

"We could have an incredible morning, too."

"Mmm. I'd like that."

Alex bent to kiss her, his hard, lean body jolting awake every single one of her nerve cells.

He was right. Sleep was overrated.

She'd rather spend her time in the Alex Zone.

Cara rose from bed slightly after 9:00 a.m. and tiptoed to the bathroom to retrieve her snow-white chenille robe. Closing the ends around her, she tied a loose bow and walked to the foyer to answer the soft knock on her door. If only she could forget all about the knock and climb right back into bed with Alex to pretend today was just any other ordinary day. Unfortunately, Cara couldn't do that. She'd have to deal with her father's mess eventually and her only consolation was that the person behind the door had to be one of five special people she trusted. All others wouldn't make it past the security gates.

She tidied her hair, took a swallow and turned the doorknob.

"Gabriella," she said, releasing her pent-up breath.

She stared into her friend's concerned eyes. Her lips were curled down in a show of sympathy. How similar she appeared to Alex in her worry.

"I heard about your father this morning. I'm so sorry, Cara."

"Come in," she said immediately, and stepped aside.

Gabriella strode toward her with open arms and they hugged tight. "Oh, Cara," she said, her voice deep with affection. "I hope you don't mind me stopping in. I was worried about you being alone last night. This is awful news," she whispered quietly.

Cara clung to her for a moment. She backed away after a few seconds and formed her words carefully. "I'm sorry, too. About what my father did to Alex. It's a wonder you still want to be my friend."

"Of course. I know you didn't have anything to do with it. And I also know how devastated you must be feeling right now."

"It came as quite a shock."

"Gabriella?" Alex strode into the room wearing only his slacks. His pirate's stubble was even more noticeable in the light of day. Gabriella's eyes widened as she took in her brother's rumpled hair and bare chest. "I thought I heard your voice," he said to his sister.

As he stood beside Cara, he curled his hand to her waist and drew her so close they bumped hips. Heat burned Cara's cheeks.

"*Dios!* You two are back together," Alex's sister said eagerly. "Alejandro, I have waited to congratulate you on your fatherhood. My brother, you will have a baby soon. Can you believe the good news?" Gabriella flung herself into Alex's arms. "I am so happy for both of you."

He stood immobilized, his arms tentatively wrapping around Gabriella's petite body. "Gabriella, what are you talking about?"

She paused, and slowly backed away, peering at his puzzled expression. "But surely you know."

Alex began shaking his head. "I know nothing about a baby."

Gabriella stood stonily silent, biting her lip, probably feeling as if she'd said enough already. Her eyes filled with apology.

Alex snapped his head around to Cara, locking their gazes. Guilt seeped out of her pores, and he didn't miss it. Then his eyes drifted down to her robed belly and for a moment he was rendered completely speechless.

Was he recalling how sensitive her breasts were last night? Did he see the slightest thickening of her belly? Her pulse jackhammered in her veins. It was time to come clean. The cat was out of the bag, but Cara couldn't articulate what she was feeling inside. She loved Alex. She'd never stopped loving him, but the gravity of his betrayal ran deep. He'd lied to everyone he'd met in Maverick County continually for two years. He'd gained trust and had abused the faith people had placed in him. Having his baby didn't change those things.

"You are pregnant?" he asked finally. His accusation was laced in a deceptively serene voice.

Cara's mouth opened, but words didn't come.

"Dios," Gabriella said on a painful groan.

"Cara, answer me," Alex said.

She swallowed and then nodded. "Yes, I am going to have a… Your baby."

"My baby," he repeated robotically as if he couldn't gather his thoughts fast enough.

"Cara, forgive me. I am so very sorry," Gabriella said. "I thought… I assumed…when I saw you both here, I believed certainly Alejandro knew."

"It's okay, Gabriella. You don't need to apologize. I had to tell him at some point. With all that's happened, I didn't have the chance to—"

"To tell me you were having my child?" Alex's voice rose to an impatiently controlled pitch. "How long have you known and why does my sister know before me?"

Pain crowded her head and she rubbed circles around her temples.

Gabriella pointed her chin toward him. "Do not speak to her that way, Alejandro. She is dealing with much. I am her friend. She confided in me. Would you rather that she not have my friendship?"

Tight-lipped, Alex retorted, "I would rather she told me herself."

The world shifted as rays of dizzying light flashed before her eyes. The pounding pulse in her head throbbed, and she staggered back. She lost her footing, her limbs going out from under her, and she felt herself falling. Strong capable arms caught her just in time. "Cara."

Alex was there, holding her, supporting her weight. His voice now soothed her jagged nerves. "Cara, my love. What is wrong?"

"I'm a little dizzy."

Gabriella spoke rapidly. "Alejandro, she is pale."

She was lifted and moved with care. The world around her began to right itself as Alex lowered her down gently onto the sofa. He sat beside her, cradling her loosely. "Call the doctor, Gabriella." She heard panic in his voice.

Cara gripped an armful of bunched tight muscles. "No, I'm feeling better now."

"But you almost fainted," he pointed out.

"Almost. I get dizzy once in a while…a combination of low blood pressure and tension."

Gabriella handed her a glass of water. "Thank you."

Cool water refreshed her throat as she sipped. "The doctor said that I need to take care not to move too quickly, especially when I first wake up."

Alex stared at her, his eyes softening. "What else?"

"To avoid stress."

Alex ran a hand down his face. *"Dios."*

Avoiding stress was easier said than done, having Paul

Windsor as a father and Alejandro del Toro as an ex-fiancé. Even Alex had to recognize that fact.

He took her hand in his and squeezed gently. "Do you want to lie down? Go back to bed?"

"No, Alex. I'm feeling better now. I have an appointment with the doctor day after tomorrow. She will check me out, but I feel fine. The baby…is very healthy."

"Our baby…" Alex grinned. "I am to be a father. It's very good news." His eyes darkened with pride. He turned to his sister. "Gabriella, will you give us a moment of privacy?"

"*Sí.* You two need to talk. I will leave now." She bent to give her friend a kiss on the cheek. "It's good that the color has returned to your face, Cara. I will call you later."

"Okay. Thanks, Gabriella."

Alex rose to walk his sister to the door, but she gestured with a wave of her hand. "I can see myself out, Alejandro." She kissed his cheek, as well. "Be good to Cara," she said. "She needs your support."

Alex nodded. "She has always had it."

"*Bueno,*" she said. "I cannot wait to be *Tía* Gabriella." She flashed a brilliant smile as she exited the house.

"She's as happy as I am," Alex said, returning to Cara. A mixture of injury, excitement and concern crossed his features. "When is the baby due?"

"In about six and a half months."

He blinked as if counting backward. Of course, he had to know the one and only time they'd been together since his disappearance was when she'd seduced him while he still had amnesia. Not her finest moment, but they'd produced a baby that night and she had no regrets about the life blooming inside her now.

"You did not trust me enough to tell me?"

She stared at him and gave him the painful truth. "No."

While they'd shared a beautiful night together, Cara had doubts about their future as a couple. Yes, they would be a family when the baby was born, but she didn't know if Alex had changed enough for her to trust him. She'd always known that this moment, when Alex found out about the baby, would be the hardest of all for her to rationalize in her head, much less explain to Alex. "This doesn't mean that we are back together."

His brows lifted. His face filled with blood and noticeable rapid breaths lifted his chest, but he restrained his frustration by speaking softly. "We are having a child together."

"The baby doesn't automatically solve our problems, Alex."

"I will not argue with you about this now. You need to rest."

"I can't rest. I need a shower, some breakfast and then I'm going to the office. I need to deal with our public relations team and figure out how to keep Windsor from tanking after my father's arrest."

Alex's lips tightened. "You will not change your mind?"

She gave her head a shake. She didn't want to leave the comfort of her home, but she owed it to her employees to show up and deal with the mess her father had made. By now, the news was out about Paul Windsor's alleged crimes. The phone she'd shut off last night would soon explode with messages. She couldn't put her head in the sand any longer. "No, I must go."

He crossed his arms around his chest and drew a deep breath as he contemplated her decision. "Then, if you must go, I will drive you. I will not let you face this alone."

"I appreciate it, but I can't let you do that. If we both show up at Windsor, it'll be asking for more chaos. The press will go wild. Right now, I need to calm things down, not make things worse."

"It will be hard to let you go," he said, as if trying to talk himself into letting her confront the situation without him. "Now that I know about the baby you carry, I am doubly worried."

"I will not place our baby in jeopardy."

He didn't seem convinced about any of it. "You won't change your mind?" he asked again.

She shook her head.

"I will help you through this. What can I do?"

She managed a wide smile. "Make me decaf coffee while I shower? Please?"

"*Dios.* You are impossible."

When she thought he would rise, he undid the ties of her robe instead. The material parted slightly, and he slipped his hands inside and grazed her skin to spread the robe open all the way. The warmth her body enjoyed evaporated as a cooler snap of air hit her. Alex's hot gaze quickly remedied that everywhere his eyes touched. Her nipples pebbled, but he didn't seem to notice. Instead, he reached out tenderly to caress the skin just above her snowy-white scalloped panties. "My baby is here."

"Yes."

His palm slid over her belly. "Hello."

Tears welled in her eyes. It was a tender moment, and Cara had had so few of those lately.

"I love you," he said to her stomach and bent to brush a kiss there. As he lifted his gaze to hers, the gentle glow in his eyes destroyed her heart.

"Oh, Alex."

"I will not hurt you, Cara."

"I want to believe that."

"I will make sure you do."

His fingers inched higher, climbing to the underside of her breasts. His touch was full of fascinating discovery now, rather than desire. "They are more sensitive than before. And fuller."

"I didn't think you'd noticed."

"I notice everything about you. Are you uncomfortable?"

"No. But I'm sure I will be as the baby grows. I'll look like I swallowed your Ferrari."

He grinned. "That will be a sight."

She leaned back on the sofa, her head propped by the back cushion. It was such a normal moment, two soon-to-be parents talking about the pregnancy. Cara had missed sharing these kinds of moments with Alex. If only she could drift pleasantly into parenthood, carving out a future minus the turmoil, deception and pain.

"I would like to meet the doctor at your appointment," Alex said.

How could she refuse that request? If it meant more normal moments like these, Cara was all for it. The doctor needed Alex's medical history, and Cara had been putting it off for weeks. Alex did have rights when it came to the baby and she wouldn't deny him the chance to ask the doctor questions and learn of the baby's development. "Okay. You can come with me tomorrow afternoon."

"No argument?" he asked with a pleased expression on his face.

"None."

Alex closed the ties of her robe with flair and rose from the sofa. "Go, take your shower. When you're through, I will have breakfast waiting for you."

"Really? You cook?"

"If you have frozen waffles or cereal and fresh fruit... yes, I cook."

"Blueberry waffles in the freezer and melon in the fridge would be a feast." She rose from the sofa and walked into her bedroom feeling a little lighter in spirit.

The handsomest man in all of Maverick County was playing chef in her kitchen.

She cracked a small smile…her booty call had benefits.

Eight

Cara escaped reporters camping out at the main house's front gates by sneaking out to a little-known back road behind her cottage. Luckily, she wasn't tracked to Windsor Energy by persistent reporters since her father was their primary target and not her. But as soon as she reached the building, she spotted local-news vans parked outside the company's front entrance and a handful of reporters swarming about.

She swung her car around to the back parking lot and pulled into her father's designated spot. Taking a deep breath, she exited her car and made her way to the backdoor, guided toward the building by added security guards she'd had the good sense to call upon this morning. Still, three reporters approached her and shouted out questions.

"Miss Windsor, what do have to say about your father's crimes against your fiancé?"

"How long have you known about your father's vendetta?"

"Do you suspect del Toro plans to retaliate?"

Protected by two burly security men, she turned to the questioning reporters and put up a stopping hand. "At the moment, I have no comment. A representative from Windsor Energy will be giving a press conference this afternoon at 4:00 p.m. Please return then with your questions."

She turned away from the deluge of questions shouted at her and entered the building. The guards quickly blocked the door with orders that only employees with Windsor badges be allowed to enter.

The news of her father's arrest was ripe, and as she made her way toward her office, she was met with questioning looks and stares from employees, some she'd known for years, some she'd hired herself and others who were loyal to Paul Windsor. Conversations died to pin-dropping silence as she strode along the corridors. Finally reaching her office, she breathed a sigh of relief.

Her assistant immediately stood up behind her desk. She had nothing but concern in her eyes. "Cara, how are you doing?"

My secret pregnancy has been revealed, my father has been arrested on kidnapping charges and the fate of my baby, the company and my sanity all rest on my shoulders. Other than that, she was fine. "I'm hanging in, Gayle. It's been a little rough lately."

"Warm cocoa is waiting in your office."

"Thanks. I'm lost without you."

"What's the plan?"

Cara liked that Gayle was a woman of action. She didn't waste time prying or probing. When she saw a problem, she dug her heels in and tried to solve it. Together they worked as an efficient team.

She sighed, slumped her shoulders and rubbed at the tension invading her skull. She couldn't grow faint again… she had the baby's health to think about. She'd have to approach this situation like any other Windsor problem, though the circumstances were dire, and take one step at a time in keeping the company's good name from floundering.

"Come into my office and we'll discuss what needs doing."

"Okay." Like a good soldier, Gayle scooped up her notebook and Cara helped by lifting Gayle's coffee mug from the desk. They passed through the shuttered windowed walls separating their offices and took seats facing each other across Cara's wide, organized desk.

Steam rose up and marshmallows drifted on top of the chocolaty concoction sitting front and center on her desk. The sweet aroma filled the office and Cara blew first then took a sip. Creamy smooth goodness flowed down her throat with comforting warmth. "Oh, thanks for this… it helps."

"My kids always needed a little extra boost in the morning before a big test."

"I guess that's what this is…a big test for me."

"Are you in charge now?"

She nodded. "For the moment." She wouldn't say it was overwhelming and scary, but she figured Gayle already knew that. "My plan is simple right now. After I speak with the board of directors, I want to meet with all of the employees this morning to let them know that despite what's going on, their jobs are not at risk. So, we'll call a mandatory meeting in two hours. Will you see to those emails?"

"Yes, I'll get on that right after our meeting."

"Second, I'll have to speak with our shareholders at some point and give them the facts. We need to assure them the company is not in jeopardy. At least at the moment. That's going to take some doing. I figure we won't be able to gather them up and get the necessary papers in order until the middle of the week at the earliest. I'll need you to contact Legal and schedule that."

Gayle nodded her head, put on her eyeglasses and began typing away. "Will do."

"And there's the matter of the press. We need to stay focused and keep positive. I need to meet with our PR reps right away and figure out the best strategy. We're calling a press conference later this afternoon. I'll write something up and have our attorney go over it before Ted Radcliffe relays the press release to the public." She leaned back in her seat and sighed noisily. "I think that's it, Gayle, can you think of anything else?"

Gayle's head lifted and she peered at Cara from above her glasses. "I think you've covered all the bases for one day."

"I hope so. My mind is a little muddled right now."

"That's understandable. How is…how is Mr. Windsor?"

"He's out on bail and lying low, strategizing with his attorney. He's been advised not to come here. The press would eat him alive and that wouldn't be good for his case. So, it's up to me now."

"I'll help you in any way I can."

"I appreciate that."

"If that's it, I'll get on this right away."

"That's it, Gayle." She lifted her mug that read Windsor Energy Brightens Our Future. "Thanks for the hot chocolate, too. It's like a morning shot of bourbon."

Gayle chuckled. "You're welcome." She rose from her seat, grabbed her things and walked out.

Cara blew out a big breath as tears welled in her eyes. Realistically, none of this would have happened if Alex del

Toro hadn't come into her world, pretending to be someone else. If she'd never met him, her life would've been simpler. Her father wouldn't have been arrested, Windsor Energy wouldn't need saving and her heart wouldn't have been broken.

But a new life thrived inside her now. Her fingers skimmed over her belly where her baby grew in wondrous little stages of development. How joyous the miracle was. If she'd never met Alejandro del Toro, the baby she'd already come to love would never have been. She would've never known what real passion meant, either, and what it felt like to love from deep within your heart until you ached from it. When all was said and done, loving Alex had brought some good to her life.

She held on to that notion throughout the day, and by the time 6:00 p.m. rolled around and the day shift had all gone home, Cara was escorted by a security guard to the parking lot.

They'd almost reached her car when David stilled and halted her from going any farther. "Hold up, Miss Windsor."

"Thanks, I'll take it from here," Alex said to the guard, leaning on her hood, his arms folded casually as if he didn't have a care in the world.

"Alex?" Her heart turned somersaults seeing him.

As nonchalant as he tried to appear, his eyes showed hints of worry as he studied her face, looking for signs of wear and tear—something she couldn't deny with the kind of day she'd had.

"Is that okay with you, Miss Windsor?" David asked.

It was more than okay. Seeing Alex here, waiting for her, surprisingly swept her spirit up and touched her soul. "Yes, it's okay. I'll be fine now. Thanks for your assistance today."

David nodded and bid her farewell.

Alex approached, his gaze touching over her every feature. "Rough day?"

Biting her lip to keep tears from spilling, she nodded.

He opened his arms and she walked straight into them. Automatically, he folded her into his granite chest, his hand gently massaging the back of her neck as he drew her head to his shoulder. She stood enfolded in his arms for long minutes, and then when she was finally ready, she pulled away.

"Thank you for being here," she said quietly.

"There's no place I would rather be." He brushed a soft kiss to her forehead. "I've been thinking about you all day."

"You were worried I'd faint?"

"I was thinking you'd need some relaxation after the day you put in. How bad was it?"

"Pretty awful. But we managed to get rid of the reporters." She glanced around the parking lot for signs of persistent lingerers. "We issued a press release this afternoon. Our man answered a few questions and hopefully now, the worst is over. You mentioned relaxation?"

He smiled and took her hand in his, tugging her away from her car. "Come, leave your car. I'll send someone for it later. We are going to my house for a little while. I have something planned. I promise you will not be disappointed."

"Alex, I don't have time for   "

"Your workday is over, is it not?"

"Technically, yes."

"Then come with me."

Why shouldn't she go? She'd had a tumultuous day and here was this gorgeous man promising her some much-needed relaxation. Part of her wondered how she'd ever relax being around Alex after the amazingly erotic night they'd shared. But her curiosity was killing her and her racked body cried out for TLC. "Okay."

Alex led her to his Ferrari, and after she lowered herself down into the seat, he gave her a reassuring wink and then gentled the door shut.

She laid her head against soft black leather, closed her weary eyes as the car's engine trembled then roared to life. One minute later, Alex entwined their fingers and brought their clasped hands to rest on his thigh. Comfort oozed from her pores.

It was the first sign of true peace she'd found all day.

"This is where I will leave you." Alex stood at the doorway leading from his bedroom to the master bath, two tall pristine columns banking him. The faint floral scent of lavender drifted to her nostrils from behind tall opened double doors. With a gesturing nod, he said, "Take a look."

Her shoes tapped against marble flooring shined to a reflective glow and inlaid with a geometric design as she strolled to the end of the hallway. Overhead in the master foyer, a chandelier twinkled with subdued controlled lighting. Giving Alex a glance first, she noted his satisfied expression before peeking into the bathroom. A tub, oversize and brimming with bubbles, welcomed her, along with a dozen burning pillar candles. A bottle of chilled sparkling cider angled inside a silver bucket and a fluted glass sat beside it. "This looks like heaven," she said, her voice sounding awed and grateful.

From across the corridor, he said, "Enjoy, Cara. Take your time. After, we will have dinner."

"Does this mean you're not joining me?" she blurted, then scrunched her face up.

Alex dug his hands into his pockets, a debate warring in his eyes. "No, I am not joining you. Indulge and I will be waiting for you when you are through. You'll find a robe in the closet."

Cara's facial muscles relaxed and she gave him a slow nod of understanding, touched that he unselfishly put her needs first "Thank you."

He lingered a moment, a small smile curving his lips as their gazes held. Then he spun on his heels and closed the double doors, leaving her alone in his luxurious room.

It didn't take her long to shed her clothes and put a toe into the perfectly tempered water. From there, she sank down carefully, and the rest of her body was lathered by sweetly scented bubbles. Surrounded by flares of flickering candlelight, she forced all negative thoughts from her head and picked up a soft washcloth to begin rinsing away the stains of the turbulent day.

She soaped her legs and torso, taking great care over her belly where her little one thrived. Then she feather cleansed her tender breasts, taking care not to overstimulate her sensitive nipples. Her hair came next. She lifted a small bottle of shampoo and poured a dollop into her hands and lathered up, weaving her fingers through the long strands. Dipping her head, she rinsed off the shampoo and once fully clean from head to toe, all tension oozed out her.

Humming satisfaction and wide-winged butterflies danced inside her. She recognized the sensations. They mirrored those she'd felt on the first days she'd met Alex Santiago when her heartstrings had pulled tight. And she knew her life would change forever. The heat was still there between them, and the sweet surrender he'd drawn from her these past few days wasn't easy to ignore. She fought his charm and charisma with all of her arsenals of defense, but tonight, at this moment, as sweet fragrances and subtle lighting relaxed her body, she was at a loss to see his flaws.

Soft music filtering in from the terrace eased her awake from a light doze. She opened her eyes to cooler water raising goose bumps on her skin. "Whoops, time to get out."

She rose and shivered from a slight chill in the air. Stepping out of the tub, she grabbed a fluffy oversize towel and patted away droplets beading on her skin. She used a different towel to squeeze moisture from her hair and then shook her head a few times. Water rained around her. Still damp-haired—her hair took forever to dry—she finger combed out several tangles before leaving it to air dry the rest of the way. She donned her underwear and lifted a lavender robe left on the marble counter and scooped her arms through the sleeves. Wrapping herself up tight, she decided the robe suited her needs better for now than the sterile work clothes she's shed minutes ago. Cozy and tension free, she blew out the candles, grabbed the bottle of her liquor of the moment— sparkling cider—and walked out of the bathroom.

Garlicky aromas sent her feet moving faster through Alex's home toward the kitchen. Her stomach groaned desperately as she sniffed Italian fare. *Comfort food.*

"Just in time." Alex opened two boxes of pizza sitting on the speckled-granite countertop. "Pepperoni and…"

"Oh, God, you didn't. Anchovy?"

"Of course I did. You love it, as I recall."

Alex was recalling a lot of things lately, making it harder and harder for her to resist him. "It's my favorite."

"There's more."

"More pizza?"

He pointed to a brown bag on the edge of the counter marked by an image of a chef tossing a pizza in the air.

Cara took a peek inside. "Mmm…antipasto salad and

garlic bread from Guiseppe's, my sin of choice tonight." Her brows rose as she feigned innocence. "And, Alex, what will *you* be having for dinner?"

His amused thick-lashed eyes dipped to the tie of her robe for a split second. "I was hoping you'd share your bounty with me."

Warmth hit her cheeks and she hoped she didn't turn as red as the pizza sauce. "Of course."

Alex turned away to set out the rest of the food and grab two paper plates. He handed her one. "Dig in. You must be hungry."

"I *am* eating for two." She snatched up two pizza slices, piled her salad high and towered a piece of garlic bread on top of everything. She walked toward the breakfast room, and a gentle hand gripped her arm. "Not in here. We're eating downstairs in the rec room."

His basement wasn't an old, moldy, enclosed windowless recreation room. It was on the same level as the backyard patio, finished in stone flooring with a well-stocked wet bar and massive rock fireplace. It was her favorite room in the house.

"That's if you don't mind watching a movie while we eat?"

"Let me guess…James Bond?"

Alex chuckled. "I wish. Tonight is all about you. How about *50 First Dates*?"

Cara's mouth dropped open. If Alex was trying to prove his love, he was doing a bang-up job. "You're not going to sit through *50 First Dates* with me."

"Is it so horrible?"

Actually, not at all *for her*. It was her favorite movie of all time. Cara loved the premise of a man so direly in love with a woman with short-term memory that he had to make her fall in love with him all over again every single day of her life. Sweet, silly and fun, just what she needed tonight. If the movie made any parallels to her situation, she refused...*refused* to make the comparison. "You'll hate it."

"As I said, tonight is all about you."

It would be great payback for the suffering he'd put her through lately. "Okay, you're on."

"Come," he said, guiding her down the wrought-iron winding staircase to the basement. "Tell me, did you enjoy your bath?"

"It was perfect."

He nodded and led her to a soft tan leather sofa. "Just what you needed?"

"Yes, you thought of everything."

She moved to the middle of the sofa with her plate and took a seat as Alex fiddled with the DVD player. The opening scene blasted light into the room, and Cara leaned back to take her first taste of pizza. Cheesy goodness filled her mouth and the tangy bite of anchovy tantalized her taste buds. "Yum."

He grinned. "You're easy."

She glanced up with an arched brow. "You don't really think so."

He settled next to her. "Pizza and a chick flick is all that makes you happy."

"Don't forget a body-seducing bath."

"That, too."

When she finished off her entire meal, Alex took away her empty plate along with his and then sank down next to her again. His arm cradled her shoulder, and she nestled into his chest. Whiffs of musky aftershave surrounded her with familiarity and steadiness. The pizza, the movie, the *man,* all combined, buoyed her spirit.

The next two hours sped by and before she knew it, the room had grown silent and dark, her head had dropped forward and the beating of Alex's heart echoed in her ears. She stayed like that, unwilling to give up the peace.

Alex didn't object. He was still, gently stroking her hair.

"I suppose I should go," she said finally.

"Or you could stay here tonight. There isn't anyone camping behind my gates to bother you. You'll get the rest you need in the guest room, if you'd like."

"Really?" She was considering the idea.

"Tonight was never about seduction, Cara."

Yes, she was getting that impression. He had not made one sexual move on her. Part of her was thrilled at his selflessness, but another small, tiniest part of her wished he had. She was at a crossroads, both in life and in this moment. "Will you hold me just like this in your bed?"

Was it unfair of her to ask it?

"Yes," he said on a gusty breath. "I would like nothing more."

"It's a pleasure to meet you, Dr. Belfort," Alex said, reaching to shake the doctor's hand over a plastic uterus sitting on her desk. Female anatomy charts and diagrams decorated the walls, and the Stations of Baby's Descent— all seven of them—were depicted on a poster behind the doctor's chair.

"Everyone calls me Jayne, or Dr. Jayne, if you'd like. And it's good to meet you, Mr. del Toro. From a brief glance at your medical history, I can tell you the baby has two very healthy parents. Everything is moving along as should be. In six and a half months, you'll be a new father."

Alex scrubbed his jaw. "I am looking forward to it, but I'll admit I am a little nervous right now."

Dr. Jayne glanced at Cara, who was nodding in agreement, sitting beside him. "It's to be expected for both of you. You'll feel better as the pregnancy progresses. Taking a childbirth class, seeing other new moms and dads in the same situation will help ease some of your anxiety. Our office offers an early-bird class starting in your fourth month. Cara has the information."

"Yes, I'm signed up to attend in a few weeks."

Alex took Cara's hand. "We'll both be attending," he said.

Cara's strength was remarkable. Last night, he'd summoned Herculean willpower while holding her in bed, giving her the peace and support she needed in sleep. This morning, she'd put on her business face and gone to work to deal with one crisis after another at Windsor. Now, this afternoon, here they both were, meeting with the doctor who would deliver their child. So much was happening all at once.

"Do either of you have any questions for me?"

Cara shook her head. "No, I think you answered everything for me during my checkup."

Dr. Jayne directed her attention to him. "Mr. del Toro?"

"As long as Cara and the baby are doing well, that is all I need to know for now."

Dr. Jayne rose and offered a smile. "If you think of anything, give the office a call. Otherwise, Cara, I'll see you in one month for your regular checkup and we'll use the Doppler. We'll be able to pick up the baby's heartbeat next time. Have a nice day."

"Thank you. Same to you." Alex rose as the doctor walked out the door.

He'd banked his anger at Cara for not telling him about the baby initially, but every so often a twinge of regret battled in his heart. Would Cara still be holding out on him if Gabriella had not spilled the news accidentally? Would he have lost the opportunity to hear the baby's heartbeats for the first time? Was Cara's faith and trust in him so dismal?

Cara grabbed her purse and stood, her gaze zeroing in on him. "Alex? Are you okay? You look like you went off the planet just then."

He blinked and refocused his thoughts. "I'm fine," he replied. "Thinking about heartbeats."

"Yeah. Me, too. I can't wait to hear it. It'll make it all seem more real."

He peered down to the tiniest waist-high baby bump under Cara's pretty blue dress. Anyone who didn't know her body intimately would never guess it was there. But Alex knew and it filled his heart with joy and anticipation for the future. "I can't wait, either. Are you ready to go?"

"Yes."

He slipped her hand inside his as they exited the office and walked outside. In this moment, with Cara by his side and a baby on the way, everything was perfect. If only he could keep her world from spiraling out of control. He stopped by the grille of his car and turned to her, taking up both of her hands and entwining their fingers. "I have an idea."

She gave their fingers a brief glance and then slid her blue-eyed gaze up to him. "I'm afraid to ask."

He grinned. "Then don't. Just come with me."

"I can't, Alex. I have so much work to do at the office tonight. Things are crazy."

"Exactly why you should take it easier. The work will be there in the morning." He pulled a pamphlet he snagged off a kiosk at Dr. Jayne's out of his back pocket and began reading bullet points. "It says right here to eat well, get plenty of rest and stay calm during gestation. Last night I took care of the first two and today I think you will enjoy what I have in mind."

Cara stared at him.

"You want to," he prodded.

"Of course I want to. Anything would be better than going back to the office tonight."

Alex dipped his eyes. The blow was sharp as a dagger.

"Oh, Alex. I didn't mean it that way. It's just that I've got major obligations with what's going on with my father and the company."

He'd ignored some obligations, too. He had put off a business trip since he'd gotten his memory back in order to make amends with Cara and his close friends. But he couldn't procrastinate any longer. Tomorrow, he would leave her for a few days. He'd miss her, and wanted to spend as much time with her as possible. "You've already put in almost a full day. I guarantee you'll have fun."

She tilted her head, her eyes filling with winsome wonder. "Fun?"

He tightened his hold on her hands, reassuring her, and then nodded. "Yes, Cara. Fun."

He was being selfish. He wanted all the time he could get with Cara. But he was also certain what he had in mind would make her happy. She needed to think about less stressful things than Windsor Oil, her father and his betrayal.

"How long?"

"An hour and then dinner?"

"Oh, so now it's dinner, too?" She smiled wide and batted her eyes a few times. "I'll admit I'm curious."

"Sounds like a yes to me."

She nodded. "Yes."

Nine

Cara stood with her feet planted solidly on the ground, closed one eye to take aim and gripped the gun with both hands. Lining up the angle, she had her target in sight. Then she squeezed the trigger exactly as she'd been taught.

A red flash of light appeared.

"Very good, Miss Windsor, you've just registered for the Universal Elite Stroller system," said Kathy, the Baby Brilliance salesgirl.

Cara stared at the complex contraption with wheels and handles and dual cup holders, of all things. "Is that a good stroller?"

"One of the best. But if you change your mind, you can shoot it again and that will remove it from your registry."

Cara's eyes darted around the massive baby store and its different departments for strollers, high chairs, cribs, bedding, car seats and more. She gave the derringer-like handgun a quick appraisal. "I really don't know what I'm doing."

Alex chuckled.

"Don't laugh," she said, pointing the gun at him. "You said this would be fun. And you don't know what you're doing, either."

He wrapped an arm around her shoulders and gestured to Kathy. "Thank you for your time. We will take it from here."

He escorted her away from the stroller section and took the gun from her hand. "It is fun. Watch." He pointed and shot at the registry tag on a wooden high chair padded in light brown and forest-green material with jungle animals. "I like this one. But if you don't, I'll just remove it."

She waved him off. "No, no. I like it, too. The monkey has a sweet face."

He reached over and kissed the tip of her nose. "*You* have a sweet face. The monkey has a monkey face." He handed her the gun. "Your turn again."

Cara darted glances from one side of the aisle to the other as they moved along the store. "Look at all this stuff, Alex. I don't know what the baby needs."

His brown eyes gleamed. "One of everything?"

She shrugged. "I guess you're right." Images of their little baby seated in the stroller or eating in the high chair played out in her mind and pulled heartstrings tight in her chest. Around her, parents with crying babies and young children swarmed the aisles. Carts were filling up fast with diapers, bottles and baffling accessories she'd not seen before. "Wow. There's so much to choose from."

"He's right, you know," a woman shopping on their aisle said, drawing Cara's attention. "Eventually you'll need one of everything." A knowing smile reached the woman's lips. "I was in your shoes a few years ago. Now look at me."

The mom stood holding her young ponytailed daughter's hand while pushing an adorable wide-eyed baby boy in a stroller loaded with a diaper bag, toys, books and baby clothes in an underneath storage compartment. "Mostly what you need in the beginning is a set of loving arms, an ample milk supply and about a hundred diapers a week."

Cara's eyes flickered at the notion. "A hundred diapers?"

"No lie. A lot of this equipment looks like it's for the baby, but what it really does is make life easier for parents. Be sure to get a sturdy play yard and a good car seat." The woman recommended the brands she liked best then moved on with her children.

Cara looked at the gun with newfound power and, dragging Alex with her, marched down the aisles determined to fill her registry. She aimed and shot, asking for Alex's opinion on many items, talking to store employees and garnering the advice of experienced mothers.

When she was through, she handed over her smoking gun to Kathy. "That was fun."

"Most new moms have a blast with it."

"I'm sure I missed a few things."

Kathy glanced at her flat belly. "I'm guessing you've got time to make adjustments."

"I do. I'll be back, I'm sure."

Alex took her hand as they exited the store. "Well?"

"Don't say I told you so," Cara said, smiling. "And you had fun, too."

"Yes, it was enjoyable. But I only need to be near you to have fun. I will miss you when I'm gone on my trip to California tomorrow."

His sweet words battered their way into her heart, while warning alarms grew silent in her head. Alex had been wonderful and supportive lately. He'd been just what she needed. "Oh, Alex."

Looking at him now, it was hard to compare the sincere man standing before her to the master of deception he'd once been. *Will the real Alex del Toro please stand up?*

Last night, even as he held her, even as he comforted her, she'd tried to guard herself from placing all of her faith in him. Yet, each hour spent with him had her slipping further away from her resolve, softening to his genuine smiles, passionate kisses and Latin charm. She was falling for him again and was hopeless to stop it. Swallowing the rest of her thoughts, Cara clamped her mouth shut. She didn't want to ruin the good mood by thinking too hard about this.

Alex studied her face and must have picked up on the tipping point they were reaching. He changed the subject. "All that shopping has made me hungry. Are you ready for a meal?"

She patted her belly. "Lately, I'm always ready for a meal."

His arm circled her waist as he walked her toward his car. "Then the three of us will eat."

"Are you sure about this?" Alex asked softly, stroking the back of his fingertips over her bare arm as she lay across the smooth sleek sheets on his bed. He loomed over her, one knee on the bed, his shirt crumpled on the floor.

She gazed at his brown skin glistening under streaming moonlight then lifted her lids to find smoldering dark eyes upon her. "Yes, I'm sure."

Earlier in the day, Cara had every intention of going home to Windsor Farms and curling up in bed alone to plot her strategy for the next workday. But then everything changed during her meal with Alex. From the second Cara stepped into the Charles Street Café, a family-style all-American restaurant that touted the best ribs in Maverick County, something uncanny, unexpected and powerful hit her with blistering force.

Families.

Lots and lots of them filled the booths. Smiling young faces and cheeks stained with barbecue sauce, parents sneaking in quick bites of their own food as they helped their little ones eat. Bibs, high chairs, joyful chatter, happy, happy faces.

Everywhere she'd turned, she saw love. She saw it in the eyes of the children. She saw it in the proud faces of parents. She saw it even as siblings bickered over toys and food. She saw it as mommies wiped faces clean, as daddies kissed the tops of children's heads.

And Cara wanted a chance at that. She wanted her child to know the love of two parents and to feel secure in that love. She wanted chaotic meals out, and sharing diaper duty and slow drives in the car to get the baby to sleep. She wanted normalcy for her baby. Was it so wrong of her to wish it? Was making love to Alex tonight a step in that direction? She wouldn't know if she didn't try.

She couldn't deny that she loved him. She'd tried to put him out of her mind, tried to talk herself out of wanting him, tried to give him up. But he was always there, reminding her of what they'd once meant to each other. Reminding her of the good things they'd had together.

Through all the good and the bad…she'd never stopped holding out hope for them. She'd never stopped feeling the powerful attraction and amazing tugs at her heart for the man who'd swept her off her feet when they'd first met. For the sake of their child and in hopes of making a life with Alex…to be a *real family,* Cara finally found forgiveness in her heart.

She gentled her arms around his neck, and he lowered down to meet her lips. Her heart was open now, free to forgive, to forget, to love again. She poured everything she held so dear inside into her kiss and when it was over, Alex pulled back slightly, his lips hovering over hers, his breath warming her face.

"Cara." He held her head in both palms, glancing at her, his gaze piercing the depths of her eyes. "I love you."

"I love you, too, Alex."

He squeezed his eyes closed as if in silent prayer. Emotions rolled over his face and Cara knew she'd made the right decision in opening up to him.

"I have waited to hear that from you again."

"I know," she said softly. "I am finding a way to forgive you."

"Thank God," he said, blowing out a whoosh of air.

Cara stroked his chest, her fingertips gliding over plane-smooth skin. She found beauty in his strength and in the way he looked at her. In the way he held her as if she was precious and treasured. A blade of thick black hair fell to his forehead. She raised her hand to brush it back as his lips smothered her in a mind-blowing kiss.

Then the bed dipped as Alex lowered down to cradle her into his arms. He pressed his body close, nibbling her throat, moistening her neck with strokes of his tongue. Her breaths came in shorter spurts now and her nerves tingled. It wasn't a booty call this time. It was real and special. Not about sex, but about intimacy and trust.

Alex slid his hand to her breast and feathered a soft fingertip caress over the sensitive peak. Cara moaned with pleasure, and he stopped, a hint of worry in his eyes. "Is it painful?"

She shook her head. "Just the opposite."

He took a relieved breath and continued to tenderly caress her, to touch her, to make her body cry out in need of him.

The rest of their clothes were shed easily and she filled her palms with his broad shoulders, the bulk of his granite chest and solid torso. He was everything she wanted in a man, and tonight they would begin to build their lives anew. Cara whispered, "Yes."

And Alex seemed to understand that the joining of their bodies was more than it had ever been before.

"Yes, sweet Cara."

She moved with Alex as one, climbing heights with measured moans and whispered oaths, finding a mirrored rhythm to his passion. He took her soaring and she hovered at the precipice with him, holding on until she couldn't bear it another second. She let go. And in that very same moment, so did he. She floated down along with him to a place that gently blanketed her happiness.

She lay in Alex's arms for long moments, smiling inside and out.

Only when she heard his soft steady breaths did she, too, close her eyes.

Her sleep would be peaceful tonight.

Cara stopped by her cottage to shower and dress for the day before she headed to Windsor for a full day of work. Hope she was sure she'd never feel again tethered tight around her as she hummed a catchy baby tune she'd heard at Baby Brilliance yesterday.

She missed Alex already. His long kiss as a morning farewell had left her wanting more, but maybe it was good that he'd be gone on business for a few days. It gave her time to think. To let the past few days sink into her brain. The whirlwind week had brought a lot of change in her life.

Maybe some of it would be for the good.

As she made her way into the rear entrance of the office, Brenden Woo, the chief financial officer of Windsor, was waiting for her by the door. "Good morning, Brenden."

"That's debatable, Cara." His mouth turned down quickly, and his normally monotone voice seemed agitated. That, more than the expression of gloom on his face, concerned her.

"That doesn't sound good," she said as he ushered her through the door.

"Let's talk about it in my office," he said.

Brenden was ten years older than she was, a trusted employee and a man who she'd come to rely on lately. "Okay."

They moved through the corridors quickly and when he offered her a seat in his office, she chose to stand. "What is it?"

"I'm afraid we're in the midst of a hostile takeover. I just got wind of it early this morning. Some of our major stockholders are nervous about the fate of the company and they've been talking with representatives from Del Toro Oil. Since the moment your father was arrested, del Toro has been secretly but aggressively pursuing the company. Some of the shareholders have already sold out."

"Oh, no." Cara's legs caved from under her, and she slumped into the seat behind her.

Unable to control her trembling, she gripped the arms of the chair. Acid burned in her stomach as she thought about Alex coming to her rescue the day her father was charged with his crimes. He'd been pretty much by her side every moment for the past few days.

Distracting her.

Keeping her busy.

Making her fall in love with him again.

Her heart bled with pain. It seeped out to seize her breath and temporarily paralyze her. Alex had to know what his father had been planning. He had to know that Rodrigo wouldn't give up on his pursuit of Windsor Energy. Everything seemed too neat and tidy, an orchestration of events that had succinctly pulled the wool over her eyes. She choked back a sob, the burn of betrayal leaving her weakened, shaken. How would she ever deal with it? How would she ever recover? "Del Toro is exacting r-revenge for wh-what my father did to his son. To Alex. If he's taken these steps already, then I'm afraid he plans to destroy Windsor."

"This is serious, Cara. He's bought up over thirty percent of the company."

Cara cared about the company, the employees who'd staked their lives on working here. For years, she'd worked side by side with her father. It had never been her dream job, but she was loyal and hardworking and she owed it to the board members and employees to try to save the company.

After getting the rest of the details from Brenden, she spent the morning working alongside company attorneys and a handful of board members, trying to circle the wagons and protect the fate of the company. She ate her lunch by her desk, taking only teeny bites of chicken salad that went down her throat like cardboard. By the end of the day, all she could think about was curling into a ball in her bed and crying her eyes out.

Later that evening on the drive home, her cell phone rang. She glanced at Alex's handsome face popping up on the phone's screen, reminding her once again of the fool she'd been. No. She wasn't going to speak to him right now. She'd been right to suspect him all along, and how convenient that he'd chosen this critical time to go out of town. With a quick flip, she shut the ringer off on her phone.

She entered her cottage, tossing her purse and sweater

onto the sofa. On shaky limbs, she made it into the kitchen to grab a glass of cucumber water and swallow her prenatal vitamins. She laid a hand on her belly, feeling the little bump. Oh, God. Her state of constant stress couldn't be good for her child. She had to hold things together for the baby's sake. Eating a little something and getting the rest she needed was her game plan tonight.

Damn you, Alex.

She grabbed a bowl of leftover vegetable soup from the fridge and heated it up in the microwave. It was the best she could do under the circumstances. As she stood over the kitchen counter and sipped spoonfuls into her mouth, the doorbell chimed, jarring through the lonely silence.

She jerked back, startled. Her first thought was of Alex. He was supposed to be in California by now. But who knew if that was even true. Her faith had been shattered today. Would he be coming here loaded with excuses? Would he even dare show his face?

Only a few trusted friends knew the new code to her gated entrance. She was immediately sorry she'd counted Alex among them.

She walked to the front door equipped with an arsenal of choice curse words she'd stored up all day just for him. How could he do this to her? Did he not care one iota about the baby he'd fathered?

She stood behind the door, debating whether to open it. "Who is it?"

"It's me, Cara. Gabriella."

Her friend's soft voice soothed her wayward thoughts. She was a del Toro, she reminded herself. But she didn't fault Gabriella her parenthood. Only Alejandro and Rodrigo del Toro had perpetrated the lie that had caused her such trouble and heartache.

She reached for the door and turned the knob. Gazing

into Gabriella's distressed face broke through her slim defenses. "Oh, Gabriella," she said.

Cara rushed into her friend's open arms and hung on tight to the shelter she offered.

"I have just heard the news," Gabriella whispered near her ear. "I am very sorry."

"Please, come inside." Cara showed her into the house and gestured toward the sofa.

Gabriella wore her hair up today, pinned back to shed light on her flawless brown skin and the dark eyes much like her brother's. The resemblance had never struck such a chord as it did tonight. "You always seem to know when I need a friend."

They sat at opposite ends of the sofa, and Gabriella turned her body to face her. "I hope you still consider me a friend." She shook her head slightly, her eyes filling with pain. "When Chance came home from the Cattleman's Club today and told me of the rumors, I worried for you. And for our friendship. You are my friend, Cara, but you may not want me to be yours any longer after learning what my father is planning."

"Your father wants to take over my company. He seems to be forcing the issue this week."

"Yes, he is a stubborn man."

"Alex h-hid his intentions well. He had me f-fooled again." Cara put her head down. If she looked at Gabriella now, she'd completely fall apart. Her heartache pinpricked every cell in her body. She drew oxygen in and continued. "I believed in him again, Gabriella. I let my guard down and he swooped in and took advantage of my weakness."

Gabriella gasped. "*Dios,* no! Oh, Cara, please do not think Alejandro had anything to do with this."

The tone of her friend's voice brought her head up, and their eyes met.

"Once, my brother allowed my father to influence him. Yes, that's true, but Alejandro learned a big lesson and he is not a man who would ever hurt you."

"It's hard for me to ignore the facts. This week especially, we have become closer. We spent a lot of time together. He kept me occupied and preyed on my vulnerability. Today, I learned the truth and he is conveniently not here. It all seemed to fall into a plan."

Gabriella's eyes widened with shock. "No, you must not believe that." She slid closer to her on the sofa, her fingers reaching out to cover Cara's hand. "Look at me, Cara. Hear me. My brother has warned my father many times not to pursue this. We both believed his urgings finally set in. I spoke with Alejandro earlier today on the phone. He is in California, as he says. He has had meetings all day, and finally tonight I was able to reach him to tell him what our father has done."

"Did he deny knowing anything about it?"

"After Alejandro cursed in two languages, yes, of course, he said he knew nothing of this. He knows you have suspicions about him still. He has promised to make it right. I would imagine he tried to call you?"

"Yes, once. I didn't answer his call."

"You didn't give him a chance to explain?"

She hadn't looked at her phone since she'd shut the ringer off. "No." Her fingers trembled down her cheeks as she shook her head, confused. "I'm afraid to hear what he has to say. I know this sounds ridiculous, but I am afraid to believe him…if that makes any sense to you. I want him to be the man I fell in love with, but I don't know if that's possible."

Gabriella's mouth turned down, and sadness darkened her eyes. "My brother is a smart man. He knows there's only one way to convince you of his sincerity. He will do what needs to be done, if I know Alejandro."

"You have so much faith in him," Cara said, wishing a piece of her heart would open for him, as well. "But what if he has deceived you, too?"

"Alejandro would not do that to you or to me. He loves you, Cara. Has he not been trying to prove that to you since his memory returned?"

It was true. Lately, he'd been wonderful, caring and thoughtful. If she hadn't already been duped by him once, she would have thought him the perfect man.

She *had* thought of him as the perfect man before his deceptions had come out.

"Yes, if only I can trust in that."

"It is not easy, but please try to hold on to that shred and give him a little time. Remember, not too long ago, I made a mistake with trust," Gabriella said. "I believed the worst about Chance *with you,* and it almost destroyed our relationship. I understand how hard this is for you, but if you give yourself the freedom to have faith, I know you won't be disappointed." She squeezed her hand and glanced at her belly. "Alejandro would not jeopardize his new family. He loves you both so very much."

"Thank you, Gabriella. For coming here and talking this through with me. I've been torn up inside about Alex. I have some thinking to do."

"Yes, but I would suggest you think with your heart. It will lead you in the right direction."

Ten

As the limo driver drove through the gates of Las Cruces, Alex glanced at the sprawling compound filled with stacked-stone archways, beautiful gardens and masonry fountains that rivaled no other in all of Mexico City. This place had been his childhood home, but now, as he sat slumped in his seat, he viewed it as a stranger would, detached from all emotion but for the chilling anger residing deep inside him. He'd flown half the night to get here this morning, thanks to his sister's call alerting him about the Windsor takeover.

Would Cara ever believe that he knew nothing of his father's plan? She would not answer his phone call and somehow that hadn't surprised him. Cara needed more than his words—she'd need tangible evidence to prove once and for all he was a man she could count on, a man she could love. All the progress he'd made in gaining her faith in him, all his hopes and dreams for their future, might have been wiped clean by his father's doings yesterday. Alex had owned up to his mistakes from the past, and he'd been trying to make restitution in every way since. Now his head swam with worry for Cara. In the early-morning hours, right before boarding the plane out of Los Angeles, he'd sent her a text message.

Do not believe the worst about me. I will take care of this. Love, Alex

The limo stopped in front of the house, and Alex bounded out of the car. "I will not stay longer than a few hours. I will need a ride back to the airport soon. Wait for me," he told the driver.

Staring at the wide berth of the double-door entranceway, he drew oxygen into his lungs and tempered the anger bubbling up inside of him. As an experienced negotiator, he knew what he needed more than anything was leverage, and he had a small arsenal to present to his father.

He used his key and entered the house unannounced, walking along the tiled flooring until he reached the breakfast room. He found his father in a plush black bathrobe, leaning back in his chair, sipping coffee and watching soccer highlights on television. "Ah, Alejandro. Why am I not surprised you are here?"

No one entered the estate without being identified, but he understood his father meant it in an entirely different way. "I came as soon as I heard about the takeover."

Rodrigo stood and walked over with outstretched arms. "First, before we speak of business, greet your papa properly."

Stiff-shouldered, Alex embraced his father out of respect. But it was a short, abrupt greeting before Alex stepped back.

"Sit, have coffee. You look tired, my son." His father took his seat again and turned off the television.

"I flew during the night to get here." Alex grabbed a cup of coffee from the pot still steaming on the counter. When the cook heard his voice, she came quickly to offer breakfast. "Nothing for me. Thank you," he told her.

He waited until she left the room before sitting down to join his father. He brought the cup to his lips and sipped. The coffee tasted strong and burned his throat a little going down. Alex winced and met his father's watchful eyes. "Your actions have hurt someone I love," Alex began. "I have asked you many times to stop your pursuit of Windsor Energy."

"It is a sound business deal, Alejandro. You, of all people, know that."

"There are many others you could pursue. It would not hurt you to stop this. I will personally make up the losses you take."

"What of the beating? The kidnapping? You almost lost your life. How can you forget what Paul Windsor has done to you?"

"I will never forget it. But your revenge will hurt me just as much if I lose Cara over this. I won't allow you to hurt her, Papa. She has been through enough. *I* have put her through enough."

"You won't *allow* me?" Rodrigo's voice elevated to a low roar and he sat up straighter in his seat. "Be respectful of your father, Alejandro. You do not tell me how to run my business."

"Papa, you are my father and I have always respected you, but I am prepared to break off ties with you. I am prepared to walk away from you and Las Cruces forever if you will not respect my wishes on this."

Jerking back, his father stared at him, unblinking. For

the first time since all of this began, Alex saw a shift in his father's demeanor. "She is that important to you?"

It's what he'd been saying all along. "As much as Mama was important to you."

A humbling climb of color rose up his father's neck and touched his brown cheeks.

"You have come around with Gabriella's choice of a husband and reconciled. Your daughter is very happy. It's good to see. Is it so wrong to want my father to be part of my family, as well?"

"I am your family, my son."

"You are part of it. *Si.* But I love Cara, Papa. She is having my child. The baby is to be your first grandchild."

Rounding his eyes, his father whispered, "You are to be a father, Alejandro?"

"*Si,* in six and a half months. I just found out only a short time ago. I am happy, Papa. I would have you join in my happiness. I would have you be a part of my child's life, but only if you stop this vendetta. I cannot divide my loyalties any longer. I cannot jeopardize my family. I have already made my choice. Now you must make yours."

His father stared at him for a good long moment, then he nodded and a small smile graced his hard mouth. "A grandchild?" His aging eyes softened to a lighter shade of black. "If only your mother could be here to see this day."

"Yes, I wish for that, too."

His father rose then, and Alex stood, as well. Rodrigo walked over to him and hugged him around the shoulders in a long embrace that seemed to settle things without any further words.

"Gayle, could you get Mr. Hollenbeck on the phone for me?" Cara asked, sitting at her desk, her gaze trained on the file she was perusing.

"It's not Gayle, Cara."

Her heart pumped hard hearing Alex's voice fill the room. Her eyes lifted to find him standing just inside her office. "Alex?"

"Don't ask what I'm doing here. Don't tell me to leave."

She began shaking her head. "No, I wouldn't…"

She paused, studying his appearance. His dark eyes were rimmed in red, the skin beneath them pale and sunken. The planes of his face were covered with dark unshaven stubble. His jet-black hair was uncombed—a first for Alex—and his clothes? They hung on his frame wrinkled and untidy.

Cara had never seen Alex looking so unkempt.

"I have cornered three cities in a little over a day to get back to you. Most of that time was spent on a plane, so I know I am not at my best at the moment."

Even in a scruffy state, Alex would still turn heads.

He didn't make a move toward her. He stood his ground, determination deepening the shade of his eyes. "When I first came to America, it was for many reasons. You know of my original motives, and I have told you many times that after I fell in love with you I had pressed my father to stop his pursuit of your company. Naively I thought he would heed my request. But he is a hard man to convince otherwise when he wants something. But Cara, believe me when I tell you, I did not know of his plans this week. I would have stopped him earlier, if he had confided in me. He did not. When Gabriella alerted me, I was in California and flew during the night to confront my father once and for all. As you now know, the takeover has been aborted. My father has canceled his plans. Your company will remain intact."

Cara rose from her chair and walked around her desk

to face him from a short distance. "How did you convince him, Alex?"

She could've melted in his eyes when they touched softly on her. "I told him the truth. That I could not divide my loyalties any longer and I would break off all ties to him as my father. I would walk away from him and never return to Mexico if he didn't stop his plans to take over Windsor. Then I told him of the baby you and I conceived out of love, a baby he would never see if he continued his vendetta."

"You had amnesia when the baby was conceived," Cara said quietly.

"I never stopped loving you, Cara. Ever."

Cara's heart was beginning to open up. She was beginning to feel the truth behind his words. She'd walked into her office early this morning to learn that Rodrigo del Toro had done an immediate about-face with the takeover. It had all happened so fast, and the good news spread quickly through the company.

"I told my father that he had many choices," Alex went on. "But only one would keep him in my life. Only one would ensure that he would know his grandchild. He is stubborn but not a fool."

"Would you have followed through on those threats?" Cara asked.

"Yes. For you not to be hurt again, I would do anything. I mean it, Cara. Perhaps I was not firm enough with my father before. And I know I have not been perfect with you. I did lie to you when we first met and I have been trying to make that up to you. I will do anything to help you right now. Please know that whatever you decide, I will support you in your decision."

Sweeping joy replaced the sadness in her heart. She took a step toward him. "Oh, Alex."

Alex put both hands up, stopping her from coming closer. "No, Cara. Not here. I have more to say to you, and I will listen to what you have to say to me, but I want us to be free of all this." A wave of his hand gestured to her office and she understood his intention. Windsor Energy and del Toro Oil had brought them together, but the two companies, and the men that ran them, had nearly broken them apart, as well.

He sounded weary and spent. She felt the same way. They needed a new perspective. "I want to be free of all this, too."

Alex gave her a prideful nod. "Do you trust me enough to meet with me tonight?"

She nodded without hesitation. "Yes."

His bloodshot eyes filled with softness and relief. "I will pick you up at seven."

"Okay."

With a nod, he pivoted on his heels and walked out her door.

Cara glanced in the bedroom mirror, adjusting layers of ruching on her powder-blue dress. The chiffon material flowed over her belly and draped to her knees in a scalloped hem. Alex loved this dress, and she was glad it still fit her around the middle. She pulled her hair back with combs after using a curling iron to add waves to her normally straight blond hair. Turning her wrist, she glanced at her jeweled watch. Alex would be arriving soon.

This was the most important decision of her life and Cara didn't want to blow it with him. After seeing an unfamiliar torment in his eyes and hearing a resolute plea in his voice, she had come to all the correct conclusions about him. Finally. She'd meant it the other night when she told him she could forgive him. And then the whole mess with the takeover happened and her faith in him had been tested once again.

Now, as much as he wanted to prove to her that he could be trusted, Cara, too, wanted to show him that she believed in him. They needed a fresh start.

She left her bedroom to adjust the lighting in the parlor. The room was tidy, with throw pillows strategically placed on the sofa. A domed dish sat in the middle of her cocktail table. Candles flickered and burned, casting dancing lights on the walls and ceiling.

Yes, it was the best she could do on short notice.

When the knock came, her nerves bunched up. She took a swallow. The man she loved was on the other side of the door. She searched her thoughts, scouring her mind for any doubt or misgivings about what she was about to do and sighed with relief when she came up empty.

She stood behind the door only a second before she opened it. The gorgeous man before her gazed deep into her eyes and smiled. Clean shaven, golden brown and dashing in a stone-gray three-piece suit, Alex no longer appeared bedraggled but handsome enough to outshine any other man on the planet. The only remnant remaining from the Alex of earlier today was the uncertain torment in his eyes.

"Cara, you look beautiful," he said immediately.

"Thank you. Please come inside." She reached for his hand and, as he took it, a curious expression stole over his face. She led him to the sofa and asked quietly, "Will you sit down?"

He studied her for a second then gestured. "After you."

They sat close to each other, Alex turning to face her at eye level. Mustering her courage and summoning the words she'd practiced in her head all afternoon, she began,

"I don't know what you have planned for tonight. But before that happens, I need to say a few things."

"Go on, sweetheart. I'm listening."

"Yes, you are listening," she said, tilting her head. "You listen to me and support me and give me the kind of love a woman can only dream about." Her voice became a whisper. "But Alex, I was crushed when I found out who you really were and your purpose for coming to Texas. I felt used and hurt and angry. It was a horrible feeling."

Alex put his head down and nodded. "I will never forgive myself for the pain I've caused you."

Torment marred his handsome face. "But since then, you have done everything in your power to win me back. To show me your love. To make me trust you again. I haven't made it easy for you, I know, and I haven't been open-minded, but can you blame me?"

"No, my love. You are not to blame for anything." The deep rasp of his sincerity warmed her heart.

"Alex, we are having a baby together. Our child deserves to come into this world with two loving parents."

Alex reached for her hand and entwined their fingers. "Yes."

"Today, you walked into my office looking beaten up in your concern for me and what I was thinking about your part in the takeover. Then you told me how you vowed to break off all ties with your father…it was a bold move and deep down I believed every word you had to say. I know you were responsible for making that takeover disappear. You put me and my welfare over your family. Something I can honestly say no one, not even my own father, has ever done for me before.

"I have been doing a lot of thinking lately. Even before you walked into my office today, I'd come to the conclusion that you are not like your father, any more than I am like mine. I cannot hold him against you any longer. As you haven't held my father's awful deeds to you against me."

Hope entered his eyes and his lips twitched.

"I think I needed that gesture from you this morning. I needed to feel like I was most important to you. I know you love me, Alex. I feel it when you touch me. I hear it when you speak my name. I see it in the depths of your deep brown eyes when you look at me. Despite our fathers, their companies and all the lies, I have faith in *you and me*."

Cara scooted closer to him on the sofa, her arms circling his neck. Her heart light with joy and a deep sense of right and wholeness, she brought her mouth to his and put everything she had into her kiss.

"Dios," he whispered, lifting his hand to stroke her cheek after the kiss ended. His gaze roamed over her face as if memorizing it. "Do you know how much I love you, Cara?"

She smiled. "Yes, I think I do."

"Multiply that by millions and you may be close."

She leaned away from him and his devouring eyes. She was not through. She had one more thing to say and was determined to finish what she'd started.

"Twice now you have asked me to give you something. As Alex Santiago, you asked for my hand in marriage and then later, as Alejandro del Toro, you asked me to give you another chance. Both times we were surrounded by nature, at a place we both love. I couldn't manage that tonight, but I can give you my answer to both questions."

She lifted the silver lid on the dish laid out on the cocktail table.

A gasp rose from Alex's throat as he eyed the decadent brownie smothered with perfectly ripe raspberries. Written in script with white frosting was one simple word. "Yes."

The engagement ring she'd taken off months ago rested atop the raspberries.

Tears welled in Alex's eyes for a moment and he took a swallow. Then he dropped onto one knee in front of her and plucked up the frosting-smudged ring. He wiped it carefully with his handkerchief, making it shine to brilliance again, and took a moment to stare into her eyes. Cara's emotions bubbled up as love and heat connected their gazes. "Cara, I am a lucky man for getting a second chance with you. I will not abuse that chance. I will always be a man you can count on. A man you can trust. I have said this before but never have I meant it more. I will spend my life making you happy. Marry me, Cara Windsor. Be my wife. Mother to our child. Be my new family."

"Yes." Cara nodded eagerly and put out her hand. Deftly, Alex slipped the ring on her finger. "It still fits," she said, a tear slipping from her eye.

"We *fit,*" Alex said. He rose from his knee and then brought her up with him to stand together. "We were made for each other."

His mouth found hers in a kiss that stole her breath and brought her unmeasured happiness. Then he wrapped his arms around her waist, tucking her close to his body.

"I have something for you, Cara," he said tenderly. "We were to go to Claire's Restaurant tonight. I reserved a corner table for just the two of us where we could speak quietly, but I am too eager to wait any longer."

"What is it, Alex? You have already put my engagement ring back on my finger. What else could you possibly have for me?"

Alex stepped back and reached into his pocket. He came up with a simple black satin jeweler's box in his hand. Her eyes touched on it before gazing at him.

He began, "The night my car was run off the road, the night I was kidnapped, I was on my way home to pick this up to give to you. I would've surprised you that night. But it was not to be. And since that time, I have waited for the right moment to give you this special piece of me."

With a gentle flip, the box opened to her. Two antique diamond earrings twinkled under candlelight. "They were my mother's."

"Oh, Alex, they are stunning." She could barely wrap her mind around the ordeal that Alex had gone through that fateful night. His thoughts had been in surprising her with such a special gift.

"Yes, just like you."

Cara fingered the box, her mouth parting and her chest swelling as she took in the delicate drop diamonds.

"It is the only piece of jewelry I requested from my mother's collection. Now they are yours. It is my wish that you wear them to our wedding."

It was another gesture from Alex that proved his sincerity. He had always truly loved her. "Yes, yes. I would be honored." She hugged the box to her chest, her love for Alex filling up every crook in her body. "I will treasure them always."

Alex smiled and circled her waist with his arms. "I want to marry you right away. I can't wait for you to be my wife." He brushed a kiss to her forehead.

"I want that, too."

Nestled in Alex's arms, Cara swayed along with him as their beautiful baby rocked and rolled with their smooth movements.

"Ladies and gentlemen, please let me introduce, to you for the first time, Mr. and Mrs. Alejandro del Toro," Deacon Hollings announced to the wedding guests sitting in attendance on the grounds of the Cattleman's Club.

Applause broke into her joyous thoughts as Alex brushed a soft kiss to her lips. Cara could hardly believe it. She was married to Alex. She returned his kiss, her heart swollen with love. "Wife," he whispered near her ear.

"Husband," she said right back.

From under an archway of greenery and colorful roses on the very spot where the new children's playground would be built, Alex took her hand and swiveled to face their friends. Above, a cloudless spring sky brought sunshine and clear air.

Gabriella adjusted the hem of Cara's ivory gown in a show of her maid-of-honor duties, and Chance, the best man, was the first to shake Alex's hand. "Congrats, brother-in-law."

Alex grinned. "Thank you."

Chance reached out to give Cara a warm hug. He'd been a good friend to her and now they were actually related. "If you're half as happy with Alex as I am with Gabriella, you're good to go."

"Then I'm good to go, because I'm very happy."

"Glad to hear it."

Alex grabbed her hand and led them down the aisle to greet their guests. Zach Lassiter, Alex's partner and his new fiancée, Sophie, stepped up to congratulate them. "No wonder I haven't seen you around the office much." Zach winked at Alex and gave Cara a kiss on the cheek. "You two look very happy."

"As happy as you and Sophie are, I'd bet," Cara said. "It'll be your turn next."

Zach grabbed Sophie's hand. They were engaged to be married, and Zach had asked Alex to be best man. Zach had listened to Alex's explanation and heartfelt apologizes and had been one of the first to forgive him. It was a blessing their partnership and friendship remained intact. "Just waiting on your man to get all his ducks in a row," Zach said to her.

Alex's mouth crooked. "Today, all the ducks have lined up. Now I look forward to your wedding."

A little tug on her gown brought Cara's gaze down. Little Cade Addison lifted his eyes to her and Cara bent down, exacting a wide berth for her ruffled gown. "Hi, Cade. You were the best ring bearer ever. Thank you so much. Did you have fun?"

"Yes, ma'am." He fiddled with the lace pillow he'd carried for his short jaunt down the aisle. "Emmie done good, too."

Emmie, two-year-old daughter to Kiley, the director of the Texas Cattleman's Club's new day-care center, made a beautiful flower girl. "Yes, Emmie did a good job, too. Both of you made our day very special."

He nodded, and Cara gave his head a loving pat before he was scooped into his daddy's arms. "That was a humdinger of a wedding," Gil said, mostly to Cade. "I'm proud of you, son."

Bailey, Gil's new wife, straightened the boy's little bow tie, her love for her stepson shining through. "So am I." Then she turned to Cara and Alex. "It was a beautiful ceremony. I'm happy for both of you."

Alex put his hand around Cara's waist. "We appreciate it."

"So many of you helped to make this day memorable for us," Cara said.

The wedding was thrown together in less than three weeks, but they couldn't have done it without the help of so many of their friends and members of the Texas Cattleman's Club combining forces. Cara had the wedding of her dreams and considered herself blessed in that regard.

As soft music drifted over from the ballroom, the guests began heading there. Cara walked hand in hand with Alex. "I can't imagine a better day," Cara said. "Are you sorry your father is not here?"

"I could ask you the same thing. I wish the situation was different for you."

"But it's not," Cara said, keeping her smile in place. Her father hadn't walked her down the aisle, he wasn't here to support her and give her his love, but she didn't dwell on that. "I can't imagine having my father here. Not after what he'd had done to you. I told myself that today I wouldn't think of anything but happy thoughts and that's exactly what I'm doing."

"Yes, that's a good plan, sweetheart. That's why my father is not here. I didn't want anything to upset our day. My father will be a small part of our lives. He will know his grandchild. But for now, it is best for us to begin our lives fresh and new. I plan to do that starting right now with my beautiful bride. It is time to celebrate."

Alex led her into the ballroom, where they joined their guests in the festivities. Toasts were made and dinner was served. Cara had never been happier in her life. When they were called up to the dance floor for their first official dance as husband and wife, Alex brought Cara close. His finger found her earlobe, and he touched the diamond earring gently. "They are perfect on you."

Cara smiled as she moved with him in time to a sweetly slow ballad. "I feel your mother is here with us today."

"Yes, I feel it, too."

"You have given me so much, Alex."

"No more than you have given me." His hand slid down to her waist, his palm covering the tiny belly bump that her lacy wedding gown hid quite nicely. Cara rested her head on his chest and swayed along with him until the music changed and others were called up to the dance floor.

Nate Battle tapped Alex on the shoulder and Amanda stood ready by his side. "Would love to take a spin with your pretty new bride," he said to Alex.

Alex nodded and stepped back, handing Cara over, and Amanda took her place. Cara was whisked away by the sheriff of Royal. Nate was an unusually good dancer, and just when Cara was stepping in perfect time with him, Dave Firestone cut in and swept her away.

By the end of the third song, Cara was winded from dancing with her friends, the men of the Texas Cattleman's Club. Out of the corner of her eye, she spotted Alex thanking Mia, his former housekeeper, for the dance. He'd had a full dance card, too, and when his eyes finally locked on hers, hot, wild sensations shot down to her toes. He approached her, moving with stealth through the dancers, and Cara couldn't tear her gaze away.

Her husband was a dashing renegade.

He stole her breath and made her dizzy with love.

"Come with me," he said. "I need to be alone with my wife." He took her hand and led her out of the ballroom and down a long empty hallway. Then he stopped as if deciding this was a good-enough place, and gently guided her back against the wall. His hands braced the wall beside her head and he began brushing long, sweet, unbelievable kisses against her lips. "Tell me you are as happy as I am," he said between kisses.

"Happier." She giggled, and he stopped kissing her to smile.

"Our new home will be ready in a few months. We will raise our baby there, Cara, and have that fresh start we have always wanted."

"I'm ready. It will be the best place to raise our son."

"Our son." Alex's eyes gleamed. Only days ago they'd found out they were having a boy. "I still can't believe it."

"Neither can I."

From a distance away, coming from the site of the old billiards room, children's laughter drifted to her ears. It was a beautiful sound. "Listen, Alex. The children are playing in the new day-care center. One day, maybe our boy will play there, too."

"Yes. I am sure he will." Alex kissed her again. "Are you ready to go back to our reception, Cara? The guests may be missing us."

"Yes, Alex. As Mrs. Alejandro del Toro, I am ready for anything."

Alex grinned, and they strolled into the ballroom of the Texas Cattleman's Club, ready to begin their new life together.

* * * * *

REQUEST YOUR FREE BOOKS!
2 FREE NOVELS PLUS 2 FREE GIFTS!

H HARLEQUIN®

Desire

ALWAYS POWERFUL, PASSIONATE AND PROVOCATIVE

YES! Please send me 2 FREE Harlequin Desire® novels and my 2 FREE gifts (gifts are worth about $10). After receiving them, if I don't wish to receive any more books, I can return the shipping statement marked "cancel." If I don't cancel, I will receive 6 brand-new novels every month and be billed just $4.55 per book in the U.S. or $4.99 per book in Canada. That's a savings of at least 13% off the cover price! It's quite a bargain! Shipping and handling is just 50¢ per book in the U.S. and 75¢ per book in Canada.* I understand that accepting the 2 free books and gifts places me under no obligation to buy anything. I can always return a shipment and cancel at any time. Even if I never buy another book, the two free books and gifts are mine to keep forever.

225/326 HDN F4ZC

_____

Name   (PLEASE PRINT)

_____

Address   Apt. #

_____

City   State/Prov.   Zip/Postal Code

_____

Signature (if under 18, a parent or guardian must sign)

Mail to the **Harlequin® Reader Service:**
IN U.S.A.: P.O. Box 1867, Buffalo, NY 14240-1867
IN CANADA: P.O. Box 609, Fort Erie, Ontario L2A 5X3

Want to try two free books from another line?
Call 1-800-873-8635 or visit www.ReaderService.com.

* Terms and prices subject to change without notice. Prices do not include applicable taxes. Sales tax applicable in N.Y. Canadian residents will be charged applicable taxes. Offer not valid in Quebec. This offer is limited to one order per household. Not valid for current subscribers to Harlequin Desire books. All orders subject to credit approval. Credit or debit balances in a customer's account(s) may be offset by any other outstanding balance owed by or to the customer. Please allow 4 to 6 weeks for delivery. Offer available while quantities last.

Your Privacy—The Harlequin® Reader Service is committed to protecting your privacy. Our Privacy Policy is available online at www.ReaderService.com or upon request from the Harlequin Reader Service.

We make a portion of our mailing list available to reputable third parties that offer products we believe may interest you. If you prefer that we not exchange your name with third parties, or if you wish to clarify or modify your communication preferences, please visit us at www.ReaderService.com/consumerschoice or write to us at Harlequin Reader Service Preference Service, P.O. Box 9062, Buffalo, NY 14269. Include your complete name and address.

HD13R

"Colleen!"

That deep voice was unmistakable. Colleen had been close to Sage Lassiter only one time before today. The night of his sister's rehearsal dinner. From across that crowded restaurant, she'd felt him watching her. The heat of his gaze had swamped her, sending ribbons of expectation unfurling throughout her body. He'd smiled and her stomach had churned with swarms of butterflies. He'd headed toward her, and she'd told herself to be calm. Cool. But it hadn't worked. Nerves had fired, knees weakened.

And just as he had been close enough to her that she could see the gleam in his eyes, J.D. had had his heart attack and everything had changed forever.

Sage Lassiter *stalked* across the parking lot toward her. He was like a man on a mission. He wore dark jeans, boots and an expensively cut black sport jacket over a long-sleeved white shirt. His brown hair flew across his forehead and his blue eyes were narrowed against the wind. In a few short seconds, he was there. Right in front of her.

She had to tip her head back to meet his gaze and when she did, nerves skated down along her spine.

"I'm so sorry about your father."

A slight frown crossed his face. "Thanks. Look, I wanted to talk to you—"

"You did?" There went her silly heart again, jumping into a gallop.

"Yes. I've got a couple questions...."

Fascination dissolved into truth. Here she was, daydreaming about a gorgeous man suddenly paying attention to her when the reality was he'd just lost his father. As J.D.'s private nurse, she'd be the first he'd turn to.

"Of course you do." Instinctively, she reached out, laid her hand on his and felt a swift jolt of electricity jump from his body to hers.

His eyes narrowed further and she knew he'd felt it, too.

Shaking his head, he said, "No. I don't have any questions about J.D. You went from nurse to millionaire in a few short months. Actually, *you're* the mystery here."

Read more of
THE BLACK SHEEP'S INHERITANCE,
available April 2014
wherever Harlequin® Desire and ebooks are sold.

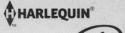

HARLEQUIN®

Desire

ALWAYS POWERFUL, PASSIONATE AND PROVOCATIVE.

HIS LOVER'S LITTLE SECRET
Billionaires and Babies
by Andrea Laurence

She's kept her baby secret for two years...

But even after a chance run-in forces her to confront the father of her son, Sabine Hayes refuses to give in to shipping magnate Gavin Brooks's demands. His power and his wealth won't turn her head this time. But Gavin never stopped wanting the woman who challenged him at every turn. He has a right to claim what's his...and he'll do just about anything to prevent her from getting away from him again.

Look for HIS LOVER'S LITTLE SECRET
by Andrea Laurence April 2014, from Harlequin® Desire!

Don't miss other scandalous titles from the
Billionaires and Babies miniseries,
available now wherever ebooks are sold.

DOUBLE THE TROUBLE by Maureen Child
YULETIDE BABY SURPRISE by Catherine Mann
CLAIMING HIS OWN by Elizabeth Gates
A BILLIONAIRE FOR CHRISTMAS by Janice Maynard
THE NANNY'S SECRET by Elizabeth Lane
SNOWBOUND WITH A BILLIONAIRE by Jules Bennett

HD73308